THE SWEETEST SEDUCTION

The Kelly Brothers, Book 1

By

Crista McHugh

The Sweetest Seduction
Copyright 2014 by Crista McHugh
Edited by Gwen Hayes
Copyedits by Victory Editing
Cover Art by Sweet N' Spicy Designs

ISBN-13: 9781940559919

CHAPTER ONE

"Next time could you please ask my permission before you auction off my services?" Lia's lecture was cut short as a deer darted out in front of her, forcing her to slam on the brakes.

"Of course, darling." Her mother continued knitting calmly in the passenger seat. "I'm just overwhelmed by how much Maureen bid. She's such a generous soul. But then, any woman who raised seven fine boys would have to have a giving heart."

Lia rolled her eyes and tested the gas pedal. The real reason her mother had insisted she cook a meal for Mrs. Kelly and her family finally became clear. Odds were ten to one that the Kelly boys were all eligible bachelors. "This isn't another one of your matchmaking schemes, is it?"

"Heavens, no." Knit, knit, purl. "You're a beautiful, intelligent woman who's perfectly capable of finding someone on her own." Although the words sounded supportive, the tone in her voice asked, "*So why am I not a grandmother yet?*"

"Ma, we've gone over this before. Getting the restaurant off the ground is my number-one priority at the moment. I don't have time to date."

"And now that it has a waiting list a month out, you can focus on something else."

Lia gritted her teeth, and it had nothing to do with the way a hidden bump in the road rattled her little four-door sedan. "No, it means I have to work even harder to make sure people keep coming back."

"Whatever you say." Her mother held her knitting project up to the light, examining the stitches before undoing the last row with a heavy sigh. "I just want you to be happy."

"I am happy." For the last year and a half, La Arietta had been both her master and her mistress, consuming every aspect her life. But her hard work had paid off. It was now the hottest restaurant on the Magnificent Mile, packed for both lunch and dinner every day. Her culinary skills had earned her a place on the cover of last month's issue of *Food and Wine* as one of the hot new chefs in America. As far she was concerned, her professional life was a fairy tale come true.

Her personal life, on the other hand...well, that was nonexistent, and she doubted any of Mrs. Kelly's fine sons would be enough to tempt her away from her passion.

She rounded another bend in the road only to see more trees. Her mother's instructions had been vague at best, simply telling her to go to Geneva Lake and then to make a right. "How much farther, Ma?"

"Just a little bit down the road." The knitting needles resumed their steady click. "Maureen's lake house is so quaint and intimate—the perfect place for a nice family dinner. And she called just this morning to say how much she appreciates you agreeing to drive up here."

Nightmares of trying to cook a four-course meal in a rustic cabin filled Lia's mind. She gripped the steering wheel and wondered why on Earth she'd ever agreed to this.

The trees finally parted, revealing a massive Craftsman-style home that looked like something Frank Lloyd Wright would've designed. Lia's jaw dropped. "Quaint and intimate?"

"Yes, darling. You should see her home in Highland Park."

So Mrs. Maureen Kelly had money. Lots of it. And Lia could only imagine how much she must've bid at the charity auction. Which begged the question of how her firmly middle-class mother knew this lady. "You said Mrs. Kelly goes to church with you?"

Her mother nodded and packed away her knitting. "She's also part of my bridge club."

Lia frowned as she parked the car at the apex of the curved driveway. She didn't know her mother played bridge. What other secrets was she hiding?

"Hello, Emilia," a tall blond woman called from the doorway. "So glad you and your daughter could make it today."

A shaggy mass of white fur bolted past the woman. Lia barely had time to grab the door before it pounced on her, knocking her back into the car. A few loud sniffs sounded in her ear before a series of wet doggy kisses coated her face.

3

"Jasper, bad dog! Come back here."

Jasper placed one extra lick on Lia's cheek before obeying his owner and retreating back to the front porch. She wiped the slobber off her skin. When she'd bemoaned the fact that it had been more than four years since any male had swept her off her feet and kissed her, this was not what she'd had in mind. "Is he always this friendly with strangers?"

To her credit, Mrs. Kelly actually sounded apologetic for her dog's behavior. "No. He's usually so well behaved."

"Must just be me, then." Lia reached into her glove compartment and retrieved the bottle of hand sanitizer she kept for those unavoidable stops at highway rest areas. It was peach, her favorite scent, and matched the shower gel and lotion she used every morning. Once she'd rubbed it into every place Jasper had licked her, she made her second attempt to get out of the car and meet her hostess.

Maureen Kelly looked like one of those women that time stood still for—probably thanks to Botox. She had to be as old as Lia's mother, but only her hands hinted at her real age. Everything else seemed to belong to a forty-something model from the latest L.L. Bean catalog. She smiled warmly while she held on to Jasper's collar. "So nice to finally meet you, Lia. Your mother just goes on and on about how proud she is of you."

Lia released the breath she'd been holding. So far, Maureen Kelly didn't seem to be a snob, despite her obvious wealth. "So nice to finally meet you, too."

"I really appreciate you coming all the way up here for

4

dinner. My son is home for a week before going to Afghanistan, and I really wanted to do something special for him."

And just like that, any resentment she felt for having to drive two hours north of Chicago vanished. "It's no trouble at all," she replied and reached for the twenty-gallon cooler in her trunk.

"Oh, don't hurt yourself. Let my son get that." Maureen turned around, Jasper's collar still in her death grip, and called into the house, "Caleb, would you please be a dear and help out your mother's friends?"

A moment later, a man appeared on the porch. He was about a head taller than Maureen, his short brown hair styled in the standard military buzz cut. He placed a kiss on his mother's cheek before jogging down the stairs to Lia's car. The afternoon sunlight twinkled in his bright blue eyes as he winked at her and grabbed the cooler. "Let me get that for you."

Okay, so maybe Ma was on to something with Kelly boys, Lia decided after watching the muscles ripple under Caleb's t-shirt. If the others were like him, they'd be a ten in the eye-candy department. But she wasn't there to ogle them. Dinner wouldn't make itself. She grabbed the remaining bags from her trunk and followed Caleb into the house.

"I wish all my boys could be home for dinner," Maureen said behind her, "but they're all grown up now and out on their own."

"Yes, yes, Mom, we're all horrible sons because we actually moved out of the house and haven't given you any grandchildren to replace us yet," Caleb replied from the kitchen.

Lia bit back a giggle. Seems like her mother wasn't the only one who'd been hinting that her children needed to settle down and start reproducing. She shared a conspiratorial grin with Caleb when he glanced over his shoulder at her.

Any fears she had about cooking dinner on a camp stove vanished when she entered the Kelly's kitchen. Sunlight poured in from the wall of windows that overlooked Geneva Lake. Granite countertops and stone tile backsplashes helped retain the natural feel of the lake house, balancing out the modern stainless steel appliances. "It's a beautiful kitchen, Mrs. Kelly."

"Please, call me Maureen." She came into the room, Jasper-free. "I hope we have everything you need."

And then some. This was truly a chef's kitchen, one she couldn't wait to test out. "It's perfect."

"Then we'll let you get started." She ushered her son out of the kitchen, leaving Lia alone to unpack the cooler.

****

Adam Kelly drummed his fingers on the steering wheel while he waited for Bates to answer his phone. As soon as he heard the click, he asked, "Any news yet on the Schlittler deal?"

"It's Sunday, Mr. Kelly," Bates replied in his ever-so-polite British accent. "Not much happens in the business world over the weekend."

"For me, it does." His Volvo C70 hit a pothole, earning a string of muttered curses about how his mother should have had that fixed years ago. "I have investors waiting for news, and I want to wrap this up as soon as possible."

"I double-checked your downtown properties. You have a lease expiring in a few months at the top of your Michigan Avenue building, but—"

"Perfect." The Magnificent Mile location would give Amadeus Schlittler the exposure he demanded. "We'll deliver the notice to the tenant tomorrow morning." The car dipped into another pothole, and he released another string of curses.

"On your way to your mother's lake house, Mr. Kelly?" Bates asked, even though he clearly already knew the answer.

"Yes. She's there with Caleb and guilt-tripped me into coming up tonight for some special dinner she won in a charity auction."

"Your mother has always been such the philanthropist." And thankfully, her donations helped lower the company's annual tax bill. "In that case, I'll leave you to enjoy her company." Bates hung up before Adam had a chance to ask him anything else.

He pulled up to his parents' lake house and checked his e-mail once more, hoping to see a message from the acclaimed Austrian chef accepting his proposal for a Chicago restaurant. Until he knew the deal was settled, he'd be popping Tums like M&Ms. Unfortunately, his 4G coverage ended about twenty miles down the road. He threw his phone down in the passenger seat and got out of the car. Dinner couldn't be over quickly enough for his liking.

A deep bark greeted him from the front porch. Jasper,

his mother's Great Pyrenees, lifted his head and thumped his tail in welcome. Adam paused to ruffle the dog's thick fur. "Been staying out of trouble, boy?"

Jasper woofed in reply and jumped to his feet, darting through the door as soon as Adam opened it. He tried to catch the dog, but his fingers barely grasped the collar before Jasper jerked free. Jasper went straight for the kitchen, his paws skidding out from under him when he rounded the corner. Adam chased after him. A metal pan clanged in the kitchen, followed by a sharp cry.

He tripled his pace, his lungs tightening, his jaw clenched. *The damn dog is going to kill someone one day.* He drew to a stop when he came to the kitchen, his fear evaporating into laughter.

Jasper was standing on his hind legs, his front paws on the shoulders of a petite woman who was pinned against the center island, his tongue lapping as fast as his wagging tail.

She tried to push the hundred-pound-plus dog away. "Enough, Jasper."

He managed to wedge his arm in between them. "Sorry about that. I—" His voice cracked when he got a glimpse of her face.

Eyes that green couldn't be natural.

"It's okay," she said with a laugh. "Apparently, Jasper seems to be overly fond of me."

Adam couldn't blame him. The woman had lips that would make Angelina Jolie jealous. They parted, the good-natured mirth in her smile changing into a sultry invitation that he would be a fool to refuse. He leaned in closer.

8

That's when Jasper decided to pounce. The dog's paws connected with his back, the full force of his weight shoving Adam forward against the woman. He braced his arms against the counter to protect her, but the soft "umph" that rose from her chest told him he wasn't as successful as he'd hoped. "Sorry again."

"No, it's quite all right. I—" Now it was her turn to suffer a vocal cord failure. Her body grew still under his. The dark centers of her eyes grew larger, intensifying the green ring around them.

Jasper's hot, panting breath bathed the back of his neck, but Adam couldn't care less. Right now his attention remained focused on the stranger in his mother's kitchen. Her soft curves pressed against him, sending all the blood toward his cock in a painfully pleasant rush. It had been months since any woman had aroused him like this, and none had ever done it as quickly as this damsel in distress. If they'd been alone at his place, he'd be picking her up right now and carrying her to the bedroom where he could savor every inch of her luscious beauty in privacy.

Instead, he was at his mother's lake house, slowly getting soaked by her drooling dog while his family watched this embarrassing situation from the doorway of the kitchen.

"Jasper, bad boy!" his mother said in the same tone she'd used on Adam and his brothers when they were children. It had the same effect on the dog as it did him, and they both backed away.

Adam grabbed Jasper's collar before he could assault the poor woman again. "Now I know why you were on the front porch," he said to the dog.

"How many times have I told you not to jump on people?" his mother chided, the anger fading from her words with each wag of her finger. Of course, Adam had been the one a little too eager to jump on his mother's houseguest just seconds before. Maybe the dog had the right idea, after all. "Adam, please take him out before he does any more harm to poor Lia."

Lia. So that was the woman's name. She straightened, a slight tremble lingering in her hands as she smoothed back the golden brown curls that had fallen around her face during the ordeal. The pink flush of her cheeks deepened. "I'm fine, Mrs. Kelly. I was more startled than anything else."

She looked at him once again, the heat in her gaze confirming his suspicion that she'd been just as affected from their close contact as he'd been. Then she turned around and began cleaning up the chopped vegetables that'd been scattered across the island.

"Come on, you overgrown lap dog." It took several tugs before Jasper obeyed and left the kitchen with his tail between his legs.

After he'd safely deposited the dog outside, two of his younger brothers ambushed him in the hallway. "Not too shabby, eh?" Dan asked.

"Yeah, Mom might have actually struck the jackpot this time," Caleb added.

Adam shoved past them. "What are you two talking about?"

"As if it wasn't obvious." Laughter laced Caleb's words.

"I'm sorry, Adam, but I don't think Lia's on the menu."

"Now be fair." Dan crossed his arms in an attempt to look serious, but the twinkle in his eyes was anything but. "I don't think Adam stands a chance, what with Jasper ready to hump Lia the second he gets near her."

"True. Adam's a bit out of practice with the ladies."

"Let me check what the magic die has to say. You need at least a seven to compete against Jasper." Dan pulled out the twenty-sided piece of red plastic he'd kept in his pocket since they were kids and rolled it across the floor. "Ouch. A five. Not much hope for you to get lucky tonight."

"Yeah, yeah, boys. Have a laugh at my expense." He peered into the living room where his mother chatted away with another woman with the same full lips as the woman in the kitchen. "Let me guess—Lia is the daughter of one of Mom's friends."

"Bingo," Caleb replied. "I'm trying hard to figure out how they were able to cook this one up, though. Somehow Mom won her at an auction."

"And of course, what would be a better way to make one of us see her as a potential wife than to have her wow us with her cooking?" Dan added.

Adam rubbed the back of his neck. As the eldest, he'd fallen victim to his fair share of his mother's matchmaking schemes. He jerked his thumb back to the kitchen. "Is she in on it, too?"

"Nope." Caleb grinned. "In fact, I got the distinct impression she's in the same boat as we are."

At least he wouldn't have to worry about Lia being

some gold-digging debutante who grew cow-eyed over the Kelly family fortune. Not that all the women his mother tried to pair him up with were. But they all had a walk down the aisle on their agendas. Was Lia any different?

"What do you think of her?" He watched his brothers closely for any flickers of interest. It was an unspoken rule among the Kelly boys that none of them would go after a girl his brother wanted.

Dan shrugged. "She's okay, but I'm too busy trying to survive residency to date anyone, especially not when there's an ER full of hot little nurses I can have flings with."

"Caleb?"

"No way. Have you seen Kourtney?" He held up his phone to show a picture of a woman with bleached-blond hair and breasts so large, Adam wondered how she was able to walk upright.

Dan's brows furrowed together as he studied the same impressive features. "They're fake."

"Who cares?" Caleb snatched the phone back and slipped it into his pocket. "I'm just thankful she agreed to move to Utah with me."

For the first time ever, Adam heard a wistful note to his brother's voice. "Serious about this one?"

"Possibly."

"Has Mom met her?"

The tips of Caleb's ears turned red, and he refused to meet Adam's gaze. "Um, yeah."

Dan leaned over and whispered, "It didn't go well."

Adam's breath caught. Growing up, he'd always known

what was happening in his brothers' lives. Why didn't he know about this? "When did that happen?"

"A couple of months ago when Mom came down to Florida." Caleb ran his fingers through his closely cropped hair. "Kourtney tried to impress her, but Mom was giving her a hard time."

Based on the picture Caleb had shown him, he could only imagine the exchange between their high-society mother and the woman who looked like she'd landed the starring role in an adult film. "If you want me to try to smooth things over—"

Caleb silenced him by holding up his hand. "Don't worry about it, Adam. I have this taken care of. You have enough to worry about with the business."

The business none of his brothers wanted any part in running. Their father had built a fortune in Chicago real estate, but only Adam had shown any interest in taking over it when he died six years ago. The rest of his brothers went on to pursue their own interests, leaving him to shoulder the burden alone. It was what was expected of him, and the big brother role was never easy to shake off. "But if you need any help or advice, you know how to reach me."

"Thanks, bro." Caleb bumped his fist against Adam's and gave him half hug. "But just to let you know, I'm not planning on proposing or anything to Kourtney until after I get back from Bagram. I need to keep my head straight over there, not answer e-mails about wedding shit."

"Good plan." Adam patted him on the back and followed his brothers into the dining room that overlooked the lake.

Lia was setting a platter on the center of the table. "Oh, you have perfect timing. I was just about to call everyone in for the first course."

That uncomfortable rush of heat washed over him as she circled the table, adjusting each place setting. The gentle sway of her hips had his fingers itching to caress their curves, to grab hold of that pert little bottom and press her close to him once again.

"Aren't you going to join us, Lia?" His mother came up behind him and sat at the edge of the table. It was only then that he noticed it had been set for five people, not six.

Lia paused at the door leading to kitchen. "Sorry, Mrs. Kelly, but I need to keep cooking if I want to get each course out on time."

"Don't worry, Maureen," Lia's mother said, sitting across from his mother. "I'll make sure she takes a break and sits down at the table for a bit."

Adam, however, welcomed the fact Lia would be spending most of the evening in the kitchen. There was no way he'd be able to eat anything if he had a continual hard-on throughout the meal.

He took a seat next to his mother and inspected the rectangular platter Lia had placed in the center of the table. Rows of bruschetta, olives, thinly sliced meats, and other Italian finger foods filled it from side to side. He held it out so his mother could choose what she wanted before placing a few items on his plate.

"What are those fried things?" Dan asked when the

platter made its way to him.

"Squash blossoms," Lia's mother replied. "It's a popular antipasto in Italy."

Images of a heavy, pasta-laden dinner flashed through Adam's mind, but the first bite of bruschetta caught him off guard. It was fresh and garlicky with a solid kick of spice at the end. Definitely not the boring Italian fare he'd had before.

"Like it, Adam?" his mother asked with a grin. "Lia is one of the top chefs in Chicago."

Despite the fact this was another one of her obvious set-ups to introduce him to a "nice girl," perhaps the meal itself would be enjoyable. He reached for a second piece of bruschetta before his brothers took them all. "Very good."

As he sampled each item on the platter, he discovered how Lia had taken a traditional Italian dish and added her own twist. The prosciutto-wrapped melon concealed a hidden stick of cucumber inside, and the olives were bathed in citrus-infused oil. "This is fabulous. Which restaurant does she work at?"

"La Arietta," her mother answered.

There was something familiar about that name. Perhaps one of his friends had mentioned it to him in the past, but it was definitely moving onto his list of places to try when he wanted to impress a client.

The platter emptied faster than he realized, leaving his mouth watering for more. It was the perfect excuse to go into the kitchen and learn more about the chef. He grabbed it and stood. "I'll go see if she has any more."

But the second he laid eyes on her, his tongue grew thick and clumsy. Frustration crawled up his spine. He'd dated models, met with high-ranking politicians, schmoozed with Chicago's elite for years, and none of them had delivered a blow to his confidence. Yet here he was, struggling to find a way to tell Lia that he enjoyed her food.

Her back was to him as she stirred something in a pan, her hips swaying as though she were dancing instead of cooking. She'd pulled her hair up into a ponytail, but a few rebellious curls had managed to break free along the nape of her neck. The button-down shirt she'd been wearing earlier was tied around her waist, the underlying tank top allowing him a better view of her smooth, sun-kissed skin. She hummed as she worked, each flick of her spoon releasing the aromas of garlic and fresh herbs into the air.

She turned around from the stove and froze when she saw him. "Is something wrong?"

The platter grew heavy in his hands, reminding him of why he'd come in the first place. "I was wondering if you had any more."

She grinned and carried her pan to the center island. "If you fill up on the *antipasti*, you'll have no room for the *prima*."

Somewhere in the back of his mind, he remembered that the *prima* course in Italy usually involved pasta. But the dish she was plating now resembled rice. He came closer to inspect it. "And is this it?"

She nodded. "*Orzo con verdure estive arrosto.*"

"In English?"

"Orzo with roasted summer vegetables." She placed a small hill of the orzo pasta with chunks of summer squash, zucchini, artichoke hearts, asparagus, tomatoes, and mushrooms onto each plate before offering a spoonful to him. "Care to try?"

"As long as there's no shrimp in it."

"Mom mentioned that some of you weren't big fans of shrimp. Don't worry—this is completely vegetarian."

A harmony of flavors sang on his tongue when he sampled it. Bright basil, rich parmesan, zesty lemon, and smooth olive oil all balanced each other out and left him wanting to grab the spoon and scrape the pan clean. She watched him expectantly, her assured smile tempting him to sample more than just her cooking. He stepped back before he lost control of himself. "It's very good."

"I know." She placed the pan in the sink and drizzled some olive oil over each plate of orzo. "It's one of my most popular dishes."

He watched the way she wiped the edges of each plate clean before adorning the pasta with a few shavings of parmesan and a sprig of basil. "Did you have any special culinary training?"

"I spent three years in Italy, learning from my aunts first before finally getting enough courage to enroll in more formal classes there."

"And is this what you've always wanted to do?"

"Not always, but once I discovered my passion, I've never been able to let go." She looked up from her work, her smile widening. "Have you ever felt that way about something, been caught totally by surprise and never realized how deep you were into it until it totally consumed you?"

Before today he might have said his work consumed him, but it didn't capture his attention and make his breath catch like Lia did. His pulse raced, not from stress but from excitement and anticipation, as she spoke of her passion. If he could only have a tenth of that passion....

He narrowed the space between them as though they were two opposite poles of a magnet, the force too strong for him to resist. "I think I might have an idea of what you're talking about."

She licked her lips, a seductive move he'd seen dozens of women practice in his presence, but with Lia it seemed to be unconscious. "Oh?"

God help me, does she have any idea what she's doing? He was close enough now to catch the faint scent of peaches that rose from her skin. His cock throbbed. He hadn't been this worked up about a girl since high school. He dug his fingers into his palms to keep from acting like a complete Neanderthal and kissing her right there.

A loud burst of laughter came from the dining room as though his brothers could see his predicament through the wooden door. His desire doused, he took a step back, painfully aware of the confused set of her mouth as she watched him. "Let me help you carry the next course out."

She blinked several times before she murmured a choked "Thank you," and grabbed three of the plates.

He took the other two and followed her into the dining room, setting one in front of his mother before putting the other in front of his chair. His mind felt fuzzy, like he'd had too much to drink even though he hadn't touched a drop of alcohol. Sweat pricked the back of his neck. As long as Lia was in the kitchen, he needed to stay out.

"You okay, Adam?" Dan asked from across the table, one brow raised.

"Yeah," he replied, flicking out his napkin and placing it on his lap. "Just peachy."

CHAPTER TWO

Lia pressed her palms to her cheeks to cool them. What the hell had just happened? One minute Adam seemed to be coming on to her, and then—BAM!—he was backing off like he'd just learned she carried the plague.

She pulled the chicken breasts she'd prepped out of the fridge and pounded them with a mallet. It didn't matter that she'd already flattened them out to the half-inch thickness she needed for the recipe—it just felt good to hit something.

Even more frustrating was her reaction to him. Normally she would've considered a guy getting that close to her an invasion of her personal space. Instead, she had to fight the urge to wrap her arms around his neck and reel his lips toward hers.

"It's just because he's a good-looking man and I've been celibate for longer than I care to admit," she whispered as she coated the chicken breasts in breadcrumbs and laid them in the sizzling pan. "I don't have time to get mixed up with anyone, much less him."

Of course, if he scratched her itch and got it out of her system...

20

Don't even go there. Adam Kelly fell into the damn sexy category with those piercing blue eyes and dark hair, but experience had taught her men like him were incapable of staying true to one woman, and she had no desire to be the *other woman*. She was better off focusing on dinner and not allowing herself to be distracted by him.

Fifteen minutes later, she'd plated the next course and was ready to deliver it to the Kellys. Once that was done, she only had to prepare the *dolce* and pack her things up. Over. Done. Far away from Adam Kelly and back home where she could dream up tomorrow's special for La Arietta.

Her resolve crumbled the moment she felt his eyes on her. He followed her every movement as she placed the *secondo* in front of his brothers and removed their *prima* plates. When she finally got to him, her stomach was tied in knots.

"This looks delicious," he said, but he wasn't looking at the food.

Her skin burned. "It is," she managed to say before her hands started shaking.

"I'll take that." He reached up and took the plate from her, his hands brushing against hers and doubling the intensity of the throbbing heat in her lower stomach.

She bit back her yelp, releasing the plate as though she'd been zapped by a jolt of electricity.

"Don't let Adam scare you," Caleb said from across the table. "He always gets what he wants and isn't afraid to grab it."

Always got what he wanted, huh? Would he follow her

21

into the kitchen again and grab her? He continued to watch her, perhaps hoping to catch some sort of invitation from her. If she gave it to him....

Nope, not going there. Not even going to indulge in the fantasy of it. She would be professional and treat this as though the Kelly family were guests in her restaurant.

She wiped her hands on her apron as though she could remove the memory of his touch. "I hope you enjoy it. Be sure to leave room for dessert, though."

"I definitely will."

Oh, dear Lord, the way he said the words almost had her wanting to offer herself for dessert. Would he continue to have that low rumble in his voice as he tasted her skin?

She couldn't escape to the kitchen quickly enough.

****

Guilt tightened Adam's chest as Lia bolted for the kitchen. He hadn't meant to scare her away. Perhaps he'd read her wrong earlier. Maybe she was some sort of reclusive spinster who freaked out when a man touched her. The idea still barely tempered the strong pull she had on him every time she entered the room.

"I don't know what's gotten into Lia tonight," her mother was saying. "She's normally so friendly, always ready to join a conversation."

"It probably didn't help that Adam yanked his dinner out of her hands," Caleb replied. "Nice manners, bro."

"I was only trying to help. It looked like her hands were full." *And she was about to spill everything on me.*

"Perhaps you should apologize to her." His mother

said the words with a sweet smile, but the tone was the same one she used when she would suggest he go to his room and think about whatever naughty thing he'd done as a child.

He eyed the door to kitchen as though it were a gateway to hell, a place of never-ending torment. "I'll give her a few minutes to settle down. Besides, I want to enjoy the food while it's still hot."

Once again, Lia's dish surprised him. It was a thin, breaded chicken breast, but she'd topped it with arugula, cherry tomatoes, and some sort of cool lemony mustard sauce. The combination of flavors and textures produced the same balanced harmony he'd come to expect from her cooking. He devoured it, sopping up the last drops of sauce with the warm bread that had been sitting on the table.

"I'm sure Lia would love to hear how much you enjoyed the meal," his mother said before he'd finished chewing. In other words his time had run out, and unless he came up with another excuse, he was bound for the kitchen.

"Yes, Mom." He stood and stretched, doing everything he could to delay the inevitable torture that awaited him on the other side of the door. He could be an adult and ignore the inner hunger that plagued him. As long as he didn't look at her, didn't allow thoughts of how wonderful her curves felt, didn't wonder how her lips would taste, he'd be fine. After all, she was just one of his mother's friends.

He opened the door and peeked into the kitchen. Lia

stood in front of the island, drizzling a bright pink sauce over little bowls of pale orange gelato. When she finished, she squirted some of the sauce onto her finger, the tip of her tongue darting out to lick it off.

Damn, didn't she know never to do that in front of a man? "Can't resist your own cooking?"

She jumped, her eyes wide, the sauce smearing along the side of that luscious mouth. "I just wanted to make sure the flavors had had time to meld."

"Uh-huh." He approached her slowly, each step a measured act of control. "And have they?"

She back away until she hit the opposite counter. "Have they what?"

"Melded together?" He was right in front of her now, desperately fighting the urge to taste the sauce lingering on her lips for himself.

Her tongue flicked out again, removing some of it. "I think so."

Before he knew what was happening, his thumb was on her cheek, cleaning away the sauce she'd missed. Her breath hitched when it traced the edge of her bottom lip. It was so soft, so full. Practically begging to be caught between his teeth as he kissed her.

Instead, he withdrew his hand and tasted what was on his thumb. Raspberry, with a hint of rum and mint. "I agree."

The tension eased from her shoulders. "I've paired it with cantaloupe gelato."

That's right—focus on the food, not her. "Interesting combination, but then, I'd expect nothing less from you."

24

The compliment came easily. His gut unclenched. There. He could have a conversation with her without being ambushed by sexual thoughts every three seconds.

"I hope your family will like it, too."

"I'm sure they will." Despite his reassurance, she still squirmed against the countertop, reminding him why he'd come back into the kitchen in the first place. "I wanted to apologize if I've done anything to make you uncomfortable tonight."

"I suppose it's like your brother said—you're used to getting what you want." A hint of a challenge edged into her voice. "But then, I should've expected that from someone like you."

"Someone like me?" He crossed his arms, refusing to give an inch until he got to the bottom of this. "And what exactly is that supposed to mean?"

"Just that. You're rich, handsome." His ego preened until she added, "I bet you thought I'd fall all over myself to get your attention."

"Excuse me?"

She brushed past him and placed sprigs of mint in the bowls. "Let's face it, Adam. We've both been tricked here because our mothers think they know what's best for us when clearly we're two very different people."

Her dismissal stung, leaving him scrambling to defend his pride. "Perhaps, but you of all people know that sometimes two very different things work well together." He picked up three of the bowls and held them out to her to prove his point.

She met him dead on with a bluntness he wished he'd

gotten earlier. "Are you saying you find me attractive?"

"I think that's pretty obvious." And if it wasn't, he'd gladly give her proof.

A rich shade of pink stole into her cheeks. "You certainly have an odd way of showing it."

"It's kind of hard when you have my mother, my brothers, and Jasper all interrupting."

That earned him a laugh. Her eyes flickered to him, then looked away. She tucked a curl behind her ear. "I don't suppose there's a place we could go where we wouldn't have to worry about interruptions?"

His cock jumped to attention, and his mouth went dry. Was this the invitation he'd been waiting for? He racked his mind for some place they could go before settling on the boat. "Care to meet me on the dock in a couple of minutes for a sunset cruise?"

"Sure, so long as my mother isn't in a hurry to get back to Chicago."

"Doubt it—she and my mom have been talking bridge strategies all night." He carried dessert into the dining room with a new spring in his step. By the end of the evening, he'd finally get to the bottom of his strange reaction to Lia and perhaps satisfy his curiosity about how her lips would feel under his.

"Everything all right, dear?" his mother asked.

"Just fine, Mom. I offered to take Lia on a quick spin around this part of the lake." He turned to his brothers and silently added, *Alone.*

Dan nodded. "Good idea. I'll have to leave soon anyway. Call and all that." He held up his pager as if to prove his point, but more likely, he wanted to get back to whatever nurse held his fancy.

"And I need to call Kourtney," Caleb said, earning an almost imperceptible frown from their mother.

Adam definitely needed to find out what had happened in Florida before his brother left for Afghanistan, but that could wait.

Right now, the closest thing to a date he'd had in the last six months was waiting for him by the boat.

****

Lia tiptoed toward the dock, scared one loud sound would have Jasper after her again. But as she got closer to the boat, a whisper of doubt echoed through her mind. *What the hell am I doing here? I'm going out there, alone, with a sexy man who will probably have me wanting to toss my panties overboard in a matter of seconds.*

In his defense, though, Adam had been a gentleman...so far. Perhaps all he wanted to do was chat.

So why did that leave her disappointed?

The sun sat low on the horizon, painting the clouds pink and orange and turning the water into fire. If Adam wanted to take her on a sunset cruise, it would be brief one. Night would be here soon, meaning she'd have to dodge deer on that gravel road in pitch-black darkness on the way home.

This is a bad idea. I should just go now before—

She spun around and collided with Adam. The scent of soap mingling with the faint trace of spicy cologne rose from his skin, filling her nostrils and turning her insides to mush. Why didn't she notice how good he smelled earlier?

He wrapped his hands around her shoulders, steadying her. "Are you okay?"

She managed to nod, even though her heart was still thumping away in her throat.

"Then why do you look scared out of your wits?"

"I...uh...." Anything but the truth. "I'm worried Jasper may come after me again."

Adam laughed and led her down the dock. "He wouldn't hurt a fly, really. Besides, I've got him tied up on the front porch, so you have nothing to worry about."

If you only knew.

"When you said boat, I wasn't expecting a small yacht," she said as they stopped in front of the sleek thirty-one-foot powerboat.

He shrugged as though it were a wooden canoe and helped her on board. "It's not the most impressive thing on the lake, but it has a small galley below if you want a glass of wine."

She stepped into the cramped room below. The "galley" consisted of a small fridge—stocked with beer, wine and soda—a microwave, and a cooktop with two eyes. It wasn't much, but it would do for a day on the lake. Of course, she didn't miss the small bed tucked into the nook at the forward end of the cabin. How many women had gone on sunset cruises and ended up under those covers?

The boat rocked from side to side, and the motor roared to life. She poured a glass of chardonnay for each of them and climbed back up to the deck, settling in the seat next to Adam. "Do you get to take this out often?"

He shook his head. "My brothers get more use out of it than I do. I haven't been on the boat in a couple of years."

So scratch the idea of taking a tumble under the covers below.

The boat glided through the water at a calm speed as Adam pointed out some of his neighbors' homes and the different landmarks. The stars were twinkling above them by the time he turned around and started back to the house. "Sorry to sound like a tour guide."

"Don't apologize. It's a nice cruise." She didn't know if it was the wine or the fact she'd just spent half an hour in his company without any of the sexual tension they'd had before, but she had finally become comfortable with Adam Kelly.

He stared straight ahead at the water. "So are you seeing anyone?"

"No. I'm too busy with my restaurant. I'm there every night, which leaves me no time for dating." *Dear God, did that really sound as pathetic as I think it did?*

"I totally understand. Work keeps me pretty busy, too."

At least I'm not the only one so obsessed with work to the point of having no social life. "What kind of work do you do?"

"I manage some properties my father built. When he died, I had to step into his shoes."

"And is that what you wanted to do?"

He shrugged again. "I'm the eldest. It was what I was expected to do."

"So? My mom expected me to get married right out of college and give her half a dozen grandkids by now, but you see I haven't done that. What's your excuse?"

29

The moonlight flashed off his white teeth as he grinned. "Okay, you got me. I enjoy the business. It's always a challenge to take what my father left and turn it into something better. For example, I'm trying to get Amadeus Schlittler to open a restaurant in one of my buildings downtown."

Her eyes widened. "*The* Amadeus Schlittler?"

"The one and same."

She let out a low whistle. "If you can get him to do that, you'd be set. I heard his New York restaurant is booked out a year in advance."

"Bingo. And it will help increase revenue to the other business in the building, which in turn would allow me to increase their rent, which in turn would increase my profit."

"Sounds like you have it all planned out. You'd be a fool to let this opportunity slip through your fingers."

"Well, it's still up in the air. I have a place that might do for him, but there are a few matters I have to take care of first."

"I hope it all goes according to plan."

A gust of wind whipped across the lake, tearing through the thin fabric of her shirt and covering her skin with gooseflesh. She shivered and crossed her arms over her chest.

Adam stopped the engines. "Let me get you a blanket." He returned from the galley a moment later and draped a fleece throw around her shoulders. "I forgot how chilly the nights can be out on the water, even though it's almost summer."

She pulled the blanket tighter around her. "Thank you."

He knelt in front of her and rubbed her arms, his motions getting slower with each pass. He grew still and stared at her. "You know, I still haven't gotten what I wanted tonight."

She braced herself for the grand overture that would involve a request for sex, but instead, Adam simply leaned forward and brushed his lips against hers in the softest of kisses. A wave of heat rushed through her, starting at her mouth and flowing to the tips of her fingers. She forgot about the cold during those few seconds.

"Now I've gotten what I wanted," he said, his voice husky with restraint.

"And is that all you wanted?" The words slipped out before she knew what she was saying, but his kiss left her hungry for more. She wanted his lips against hers again, his arms around her, his body pressed against hers while he kissed her until she grew dizzy from holding her breath.

"I didn't want to presume too much."

"I appreciate that." She threaded her fingers through his hair and pulled him toward her until their lips met again.

This time there was nothing sweet and hesitant about the kiss. She gladly opened her mouth to him when his tongue swept along the seam and clung to him as he took her to that head-spinning state she craved. The blanket slipped from her shoulders, followed by her button-down shirt, leaving her in the thin-strapped, cami-style tank top.

His hands chased away any of the cold that threatened

31

her bare skin, caressing her arms, her shoulders. His lips followed, blazing a trail of heat along her neck and down her chest. One of the straps fell off her shoulder, followed by a tug along her neckline that allowed him access to her breast. He ran his thumb across the taut peak, teasing it for a second before taking it into his mouth.

A moan rose from her mouth as Adam alternated between using his teeth and his tongue on the sensitive bit of flesh. She slid out of her chair and straddled his lap, pressing her body against his. The hard ridge of his cock through his jeans both delighted and tormented her. She rocked against him, encouraging him to continue.

"Oh, God, Lia." He grabbed her hips and held her still. His lips abandoned her breast and devoured her mouth once again until they were both left gasping for air. "You taste more delicious than I could've imagined."

"Then don't stop," she urged before she lost her courage. Maybe she didn't have time to date, but she wasn't going to turn down what could possibly be the best sex in her life if the foreplay was any indication.

His t-shirt came off in an instant, followed by her tank top. The coarse hair on his chest scratched against her already-tender nipples. Her sex clenched each time his tongue danced around hers, each time his hands ran down her back, each time he ground his erection against her. If she wasn't careful, she'd be coming before he even got inside her.

His fingers hooked the waist of her jeans. His kisses quickened, revealing his desire was just as desperate as hers. He reached behind her for the blanket and wrapped it around her bare back before lowering her to the deck. Then, with what had to be well-practiced skill, he unzipped her jeans and worked his hand into her panties.

She moaned his name when he found her clit, unable to say anything else in her drunken haze of lust. He varied the pressure of his strokes, sliding from the tiny nub down to the deeper recess of her sex. Each movement drew her closer and closer to the brink, to the point of release.

But instead of a blinding orgasm, she got a blinding spotlight in the face, followed by a voice across a bullhorn saying, "Is anyone on board?"

Adam cursed and wrapped the blanket around her bare chest, moving between her and the police boat's searchlight. "We're fine, Bob. Just stopped the boat for a moment."

Lia wanted nothing more than to vaporize right there on the deck. If she and Adam had been a couple of horny teenagers, getting caught by the cops wouldn't have been so mortifying. But they were adults, and the police had probably gotten more than an eyeful of her as she'd writhed around half-naked under Adam moments before.

"Just wanted to make sure, Adam," Bob the police officer said, this time without the bullhorn. "Say hi to your mother for me."

"Will do." Adam gave him a salute as the police boat pulled away from them. Once they were back in the dark, he sat beside her and ran his fingers through his hair to smooth it out. "Well, that was embarrassing."

"To say the least." Any desire she'd felt had vanished. She searched the deck for her clothes.

"Perhaps we should head back." Adam grabbed her tank top and shirt. "Here, put these on before Bob makes his next pass."

She was fully dressed in less than a minute, the blanket wrapped securely around her once again.

Adam started the engine and drove the boat back to his mother's lake house in silence. Disappointment gnawed deep inside her. If the cops hadn't shown up, their bodies would probably be tangled in post-coital bliss by now. Instead, he refused to even look at her, leaving her with more questions than ever. Was he truly interested in her? Or was he just looking to score? If she knew where she stood with him, then maybe she could figure out what she wanted to do next.

The boat slowed down as it approached the dock. Adam slipped past her and tied the boat to the moorings. When she tried to leave, he blocked her. "I'm really sorry Bob barged in on us like that."

"It happens," she said, anxious for the night to end.

He cupped her chin so she was forced to look at him. "What I meant to say is that I had a good time, and I'd like to see you again."

"I thought you said you were too busy to date."

"I am, but I could make time for you if you'd be willing to make time for me." He released her chin and pulled her into his arms. "That is, if you want to see me again."

How could she say no when her body was already craving wicked things with his? "I think I could find some time for you."

"That's just what I wanted to hear." He gave her a

cocky grin before lowering his mouth to hers once again.

Lia laughed in spite of herself. Adam apparently did always get what he wanted, and she'd fallen right into his hands. Of course, if those hands continued what they'd started on the boat, then she was in for a fun ride while it lasted.

Two deep barks came from the house, and a flash of white raced along the dock toward them. Lia's muscles locked, preparing for Jasper's impact.

"No, no!" Adam moved in front of her to shield her from the Great Pyrenees. "Down, boy!"

But Jasper refused to listen. He pounced on them. Lia stumbled back. Her foot hit air. Then the cold water of the lake enveloped her.

CHAPTER THREE

Adam drummed his finger against the back of his iPad while Bates navigated traffic along Michigan Avenue. Last night had been a disaster of epic proportions, but once he retrieved Lia from the lake, she'd still been willing to give him her phone number. She'd even entered it into his phone so he wouldn't lose it. Not that he would. He'd never had a woman turn him on like she did. One kiss, and he was gone.

"I apologize for the traffic, Mr. Kelly. We should be there in a few minutes."

"Take your time, Bates. I'm just thinking about other things." Like when he should call Lia. As much as he itched to finish what they'd started last night, he didn't want to appear to be a complete sleaze who was only interested in sex. Not that he didn't want it. But he also enjoyed her company enough to be willing to carve out time in his busy schedule for her, and that said a lot.

And he wanted to make time for her—almost as much as he wanted Amadeus Schlittler to open a restaurant in his building.

"The space I mentioned yesterday is already occupied

by a restaurant, so Mr. Schlittler will have no trouble converting it to his needs."

"Good to know." And even better that Bates had already scouted out the location for him and seen to all the details. "You said the tenant only had a couple of months left on the lease?"

"Yes, sir. She's subleasing the space after that dessert bar was forced to close, and has requested her own lease. Even though you're not going to offer it to her, I'm sure she'll appreciate the fact you wanted to deliver the news personally."

"If I'm not going to renew her lease, I suppose she'll want to know why." He shifted in his seat. Confrontations always made him edgy, but he'd learned over the years that it was better to deliver bad news in person and then point tenants to his staff to handle any of their concerns. It was messy up front, but almost always resulted in a good outcome in the end. "What's her name again?"

"Ms. Mantovani."

He shifted in his seat again. The Italian name resurrected his memories of Lia and how she'd murmured naughty-sounding things in that language while his tongue swirled around her sweet little nipple. His cock stiffened, and he pulled out his phone, wondering how much time would need to pass before it was safe to call her.

Bates turned into the parking garage under the building and keyed in his entry code.

Adam adjusted his tie and erased Lia from his mind. He didn't need to go into a meeting with a tent pole in his pants.

An elevator took them from the parking garage to the lobby. This was the last building his father had commissioned, but he'd died four months before it was finished. Still, Adam saw little pieces of his father in the building, from the marble tile to the rich mahogany of the receptionist's desk. But since it was also the first property Adam had completed as head of the family business, he'd added his own touches to it, such as the Chihuly glass sculptures that hung from the lobby's ceiling three stories above. If he had his choice, he'd leave the day-to-day details of the family business to Bates so he could focus on creating new properties and reviving his current ones with fresh ideas.

Bates pushed the button for the elevator that would take them to the top of the tower. The spectacular views would only enhance Amadeus's cooking. In other words, it was perfect. He glanced at Bates and tried to read anything from the man's stoic expression. "Did Chef Schlittler seem pleased when you mentioned this space to him?"

"Yes, sir, but he still wants to inspect it personally next week." Then, with an uncharacteristic tug of his collar, Bates added, "Mr. Kelly, are you sure you want to evict the current tenant? Ms. Mantovani has done an outstanding job of creating a restaurant here already, and she has established this as one of the hottest reservations in town in such a short time."

"She's not Amadeus Schlittler."

The elevator dinged, and the doors parted to let them enter. As the elevator zoomed to the top, Bates continued,

"Perhaps it would be wiser to invest in local talent rather than bring in a big name."

"A big name will generate more interest, and therefore more money, than a relative unknown." He tightened his hand into a fist. "This is business, Bates. Don't let it get personal. I've made my mind up, and nothing is going to change it."

"Of course, sir. I was just merely making a suggestion."

The elevator stopped, and the doors opened into an entryway that reminded him of a Tuscan villa, right down to the cracked plaster. Not something Amadeus would like if the décor of his current restaurants was any indication. Adam's mind immediately started calculating the cost to have it removed.

As he scanned the walls, he spotted a framed cover of last month's *Food and Wine* talking about the hottest new chefs in America. And right in the center of the photo was a breaded chicken breast with an arugula salad on top. His stomach dropped. "What was the name of this restaurant again?"

"La Arietta," Bates replied.

His mouth went dry, and his palms grew damp. *Shit!*

"Come along, Mr. Kelly." Bates opened the front door to the dining room. "I expect Ms. Mantovani would like to hear your news before the lunch rush."

The waitstaff inside froze as he and Bates entered the room. A thin man with overly-gelled black hair and a gray suit approached them. "Ah, Mr. Bates, so good to see you again."

If the slightly feminine tone to the man's words didn't

clue Adam into the man's sexuality, the black eyeliner sealed the deal.

"Good to see you, too, Dax. I hope we're catching Ms. Mantovani at a good time."

"Please," Dax said with a huff and jutted his hip out. "The girl never leaves this place. I'll get her for you."

Once Dax disappeared into the kitchen, Bates cleared his throat. "Dax is the maître d'," he said as though that explained everything.

Adam offered a silent prayer to whatever deity might be listening that this was all just a bad dream, that this was not Lia's restaurant.

The gods weren't on his side.

The chef who emerged from the kitchen had the same golden brown curls, the same bright green eyes, the same luscious lips as the woman he'd almost slept with last night. Her smile faded when she saw him. "Adam, what are you doing here?"

Shit, shit, shit, shit!

Bates's gaze travelled between them. "You two know each other?"

"We met yesterday at his mother's lake house."

Adam tried to form coherent words, but his mind was still populating four-letter words. How the hell did someone like Lia land one of the hottest real estate venues in Chicago?

When he continued to remain speechless, Bates stepped in. "Mr. Kelly wanted to speak to you about your lease."

The corners of her mouth twitched higher into a

nervous smile. "I'm ready to sign the renewal whenever you are. As you may have heard, business is booming here."

It was time to end this agony as quickly as possible. "I'm not renewing your lease."

There. He said it. Now he was ready to be damned to hell and suffer whatever punishment awaited him.

The color drained from Lia's face. "Not renewing my lease?" Her bottom lip trembled. "Why?"

In took every ounce of strength not to take her into his arms and comfort her, but he needed to stay in control if he wanted his plan to go smoothly. "Amadeus Schlittler wants to open his restaurant here."

Her disbelief faded into barely contained rage. The tremulous tone in her voice revealed how hard she fought not to scream at him. "You're evicting me for *him*?"

"You said it yourself last night—I'd be a fool to let this opportunity slip through my fingers." The stark emotion of his words rattled him. He sounded like a complete dick.

Her nostrils flared and the bottom lid of her right eye twitched, but she remained rigidly still otherwise. Her mouth opened and snapped shut several times. Finally she said, "Well, I have two months left on my sublease, and I'm not leaving until then."

Lia spun around on her heel and marched into the kitchen, her back and arms still ramrod straight. Her flamboyant maître d' backpedaled several feet before following her. The rest of the wait staff all glared at him as though he'd just kicked the crutch out from under Tiny Tim.

The room temperature seemed to have jumped twenty degrees too high for his comfort. "Let's go, Bates."

"Yes, Mr. Kelly." He waited until they were safely in the elevator before saying, "I take it you were unaware she was your tenant."

"Completely unaware. I don't remember her name on the lease." If he'd known that, he would have stayed the hell away from her last night. Rule number one was never to mix business with pleasure, and he'd already more than overstepped that boundary.

"It was a sublease, sir. And are still certain you want to evict her in favor of Mr. Schlittler?"

Doubt wormed through him, making him pause a second. "What's done is done, Bates. The Schlittler deal is contingent on him getting this space. He's the chef my investors want and there's nothing I can do about it."

Bates cleared his throat again. "That's a pity, sir. Ms. Mantovani has proven to be an ideal tenant."

And one helluva kisser, but that didn't change things. "Please inform Mr. Schlittler that the space will be his on the first of next month."

****

Lia barged straight through the kitchen and into her office. Her lungs burned for air, and her chest heaved at an unnatural rate. A sob choked her throat. What the hell just happened?

Julie, her sous chef, peeked in. Worry replaced her normally cheerful smile. "Dax, honey, get Lia a shot of grappa."

Lia opened her mouth to tell Julie that wasn't necessary

but instead what came out was, "That fucking asshole!"

"Uh-oh, better make that two shots of grappa." Julie came in and closed the door behind her. "Calm down, sweetie, and tell me what's going on."

Lia sank down onto her desk chair and pressed her palms against her eyes. "I can't believe I almost slept with him."

"Ooh, sounds like I'm just in time for the juicy details." Dax set two glasses on her desk. "Are you talking about Mr. Tall, Dark, and Handsome?"

Julie popped him with the back of her hand. "This is serious. Now, start from the beginning, Lia."

"You know how my mom auctioned off a meal cooked by me last month at the charity thing? Well, the winner was Adam's mom."

"And Adam is that fine-looking specimen in a suit?" Dax practically drooled. "So did dessert take on a whole different meaning? Not that I blame you."

"After dinner, he took me out on the boat, and...." As angry as she was at him, her sex still clenched when she remembered last night. "Well, one thing led to another."

Julie sat down on the desk and handed her the first shot. "You said you almost slept with him—what kept you from going all the way?"

"A police officer with a very bright spotlight." Lia took the glass and downed the bitter liquor in a single gulp. It matched her mood. "I wouldn't be surprised if he was trying to seduce me so I wouldn't be so upset when he dropped this bomb on me."

"Speaking from a guy's perspective, you've got it all

backward. You drop the bomb first, then offer the condolence sex." Dax nudged the second glass of grappa toward her. "But let's look on the bright side—you still have an ace up your sleeve."

Lia took a sip, letting the fiery grappa burn its way down into her stomach and calm her anger. "What do you mean? You heard him—he's kicking me out for Amadeus Schlittler."

"Yes, but you have the one thing Amadeus Schlittler doesn't have." Dax wrapped his arm around her shoulder and hugged her. "Well, three things, if you count your tits."

Julie puckered her mouth like she'd just bit into a lemon. "You did not just go there."

"Oh, yes, I did." Dax snapped his fingers in front of Julie's face. "If Lia wants to keep this place, then she needs to go to Mr. Suit and work it."

Lia slammed her glass on the desk. "I'm not going to stoop to that level. If Adam wants to shut down La Arietta and kick me out, then fine. But I'm not going to sleep with him to keep this location."

"I'll sleep with him," Dax volunteered. "I don't pretend to have any morals as far as hot men are concerned."

"You are such a slut." Julie gave Dax a playful shove. "But seriously though, have you thought about using your feminine wiles to your advantage? I mean he seemed to be into you last night, right?"

Lia nodded, the irony of last night's events mocking her. "He even asked for my phone number."

"Then maybe when he calls, you let him know how

much this restaurant means to you. Win him over to your side. Flirt, if you need to."

"Suck his dick, if you need to," Dax said with a grin, earning another smack from Julie.

Lia massaged her temples. "I love La Arietta, but I'm not going to stoop to prostitution to keep her. Besides, Adam is a businessman. The only way I'm going to change his mind is to show him that I'd do a better job of increasing his bottom line than Amadeus Schlittler."

"And if you need help grabbing his bottom line, I'll be more than happy to assist." Dax hugged her again, growing serious. "Oh, sweetheart, I'm so sorry you're having to deal with this. What can I do to help?"

Lia stood up and adjusted her chef's jacket. "Make sure that we're booked to maximum capacity every night. If he sees a line out the door, then he'll know we're making a profit."

Julie hopped off the desk. "And what can I do?"

"Help me create some new dishes that will have people talking." She opened the office door and saw her kitchen staff already prepping for the day's meals. "Maybe we can even contact one of the local news programs and do a cooking demonstration."

"Or maybe you can go on the news and get the people upset by telling them we're being forced to close," Julie suggested.

She stared at her kitchen, her gaze panning from one end to the other. This was her home, her dream, her true love. How far would she be willing to go to keep it? A lump rose into her throat. "If I have to do that, I will. But for now, let's try to be civil."

CHAPTER FOUR

Lia sprinkled thin ribbons of basil into the sauté pan while she flipped the linguine in the white wine and olive oil sauce. The Thursday night dinner rush was in full swing, and she wanted to make sure that every tiny detail was perfect. "Is that halibut ready?" she asked Julie.

"Coming off the grill now."

Lia shimmied the pasta onto a clean plate, waited for Julie to top it with the fish, and then drizzled some of the remaining sauce on top. A few more shreds of basil for garnish, a quick wipe of the plate's brim, and it was ready to go. "I need a runner."

A member of her wait staff snatched the plate and disappeared into the dining room.

Dax appeared as the door swung back in. "You'll never believe who just showed up and asked for a table without a reservation."

Lia tossed the dirty pan in the sink and grabbed a clean one. "I don't have time for guessing games."

"Oh, but I think you'll enjoy this." He dragged her over to the window looking out into the dining room and pointed to a couple sitting at a corner table.

47

Lia didn't recognize the woman, but there was no mistaking Adam Kelly. They were sitting next to each other, their heads bent in deep conversation. "He brought a date here?"

"That's some nerve," Julie said from over her shoulder while she whisked a fresh batch of vinaigrette. "Why did you seat them, Dax?"

"Because we had a last minute cancellation." He pushed them away from the door as a waiter approached. "Don't you two see? This is Lia's chance to wow him with her cooking *and* make him look like a total shit in front of his date when she learns he's closing this place down. It's brilliant!"

Or I can just walk out there and whack him in the back of the head with this frying pan. The idea tempted her more than she cared to admit. She spun the pan around in her hand and weighed the consequences of her actions.

Unfortunately, Dax had the better plan. "Okay, fine, let him eat. In fact, I'm going to prepare a special treat for him and his date. Luis, take over on the pasta station."

Dax dashed back into the dining room while Julie followed Lia over to a small workstation. "What do you have in mind?"

Lia held up two large prawns. "I have it on good authority that Mr. Kelly isn't fond of shrimp. Maybe it's time I changed his mind."

****

"So what do you think of this place so far, Vanessa?" Adam asked as the waiter cleared the plates from their *prima* course.

48

She wiped the corners of her mouth with a napkin before replying in her posh British accent, "I would describe it as bold and inventive."

"Tell me what you really think."

All pretense dropped, and the food critic next him relaxed into the girl from Ipswich he'd befriended years ago at Oxford. "It's bloody good, that's what it is. I almost need a cigarette after that orgasmic risotto. Where did you find this place? It should be a must eat for anyone visiting Chicago."

Adam shifted in his seat. If he could survive this conversation without admitting that he was in the process of shutting La Arietta down, he'd have to go out and by a lottery ticket. "I own this building, remember?"

"Well, it was a brilliant idea to open this place." She fished around in her handbag for a tube of lipstick and a mirror. "Do anything you can to keep the owner because she's going to be a star by the time I write this place up."

He folded his hands together and cursed under his breath. "Actually, Amadeus Schlittler will be opening up a restaurant here soon."

Vanessa froze, her lipstick hovering over her lips. "Please tell me you're joking."

Before he had a chance to answer, two waiters came with the meat course. Vanessa, being the foodie she was, had demanded they order five different entrees so they could sample them all. Adam made sure Lia's Chicken Milano was one of them.

Vanessa put away her lipstick and placed her napkin back in her lap, but her glare was still firmly in place.

49

"Adam?"

He stabbed the filet mignon with his fork and cut into it, his knife sliding through the tender meat like it was butter. "You should try the chicken."

"Adam?" Her voice took on a feral growl, the one she reserved whenever someone got between her and her food. How she managed to keep such a trim figure amazed him.

"Can I pour you another glass of wine?"

She pried the bottle out of his hand. "What the fuck are you thinking?"

He laid his utensils on his plate and leaned back. The battle was lost. "He's a bigger draw that the current owner. If I can get him here, then I can increase the rent on the other spaces in this building."

"Amadeus Schlittler is a complete wanker who lost any culinary creativity decades ago. I wouldn't be caught dead in one his restaurants, even if it was last place on Earth serving hot food." She emptied the bottle into her glass and took a long drink. "You're a fucking idiot if you think you're better off closing this place down for him."

He closed his eyes and took a deep breath. Vanessa just confirmed the doubt that had been eating away at him all week. "Then what do you suggest I do?"

"Tell Schlittler to piss off and marry this goddess." She took a bite of the Chicken Milano and gave a moan of pure ecstasy that none of her lovers had probably ever extracted from her. "I'm serious."

If she only knew how close she came to striking a nerve. He'd lost count how many times he'd pulled his phone out and stared at the number Lia had entered on Sunday. The problem was he didn't know what he'd say to her if she answered his call. And none of it had anything to do with business. "I think it's a little late for that. She hates me."

"Now whatever gave you that idea?" a familiar voice said behind him. He turned around and found Lia standing there, holding a small plate in her hands.

His tongue stumbled in his mouth like a drunken frat boy. Thankfully, Vanessa came to his rescue. She extended her hand to Lia, her posh accent back in place. "You must be the genius behind every delectable dish we've been served this evening."

"I am. Thank you." Lia shook Vanessa's hand, but remained cool and aloof. Her eyes slid to Adam as she added, "I'm very glad to hear you've been enjoying your meal."

He didn't miss the thinly veiled message behind her words. If she wanted him to know her cooking was top notch, her point had been made this weekend. The crowded dining room just confirmed her skill.

"And what do we have here?" Vanessa asked, pointing to the plate in Lia's hands.

"It's a new dish I've been working on. I thought I'd let you two try it first and tell me what you think." She placed the plate with two small golden brown pinwheels and front of him and waited.

Vanessa wasted no time sampling it, praising it with another one of her sex kitten moans. "Oh my God, Adam, you have to try this."

Lia crossed her arms and lifted her chin, daring him to take a bite.

He picked up his fork, his eyes never leaving her, and pressed it into the other pinwheel. The outside crunched, letting him know it had been fried, but the inside was soft and warm. He took a bite. The rich, gooey filling was a mixture of creamy ricotta, roasted garlic, and a hint of something sweet that he couldn't name. Now he knew why Vanessa had rewarded it with one her trademarked moans. It was fabulous. He devoured the rest in three quick bites.

"Like it?" Lia asked with a smirk.

He coughed and wiped his mouth with his napkin. "Yes, it's very good. But then you knew that."

Her grin widened. "And now you know it, too. Good evening."

She turned to leave, but Vanessa stopped her. "A moment, please. What do you call this treat?"

Lia stared directly at him and replied, "*Lasagne fritti con gamberi e aragosta.*" She returned to the kitchen before he had a chance to ask her to translate.

Vanessa dove into the next entree. "Abso-fucking-lutely brilliant."

He took a gulp of wine to soothe the tickle in his throat and congratulated himself on getting through an awkward situation. "That went well."

"Yes, if you leave out the part where she looked she wanted to skewer me." She came back to the chicken and took another bite. "Why do I have the sneaking suspicion there's more to you two than what you're telling me?"

The back of his neck itched. "Because there is."

"Out with it." Vanessa chewed and waited, knife and fork still in hand.

"It's a bit of a comedy of errors."

"Let me guess—you shagged her and didn't know she was one of your tenants."

Now the itch had moved to between his shoulder blades. He rubbed his back against his chair. "Not exactly, but close."

"Close what? Close in that you almost shagged her? Or close in that you didn't know who she was?"

"Both."

The knife and fork fell to Vanessa's plate with a clang. "You've gotten yourself into a bloody mess, haven't you?" She crossed her arms on the table. "Now, what are you going to do about it?"

He dug his fingers into his palms to keep from clawing at his thighs, they itched so much. Being under the scrutiny of one of his oldest friends while in a wool suit was anything but comfortable. "What can I do? I can't mix business with pleasure."

"Don't be a complete nutter. You know as well as I do that you were never one for playing by the rules."

"That was then, and this is now." He rocked from side to side, soothing the burning across his lower back. "I doubt she'll have anything to do with me unless I promise to let her keep the restaurant."

"And that would be a bad thing how? Think about it, Adam. You'd still have a top notch chef working here, and you'd be shagging a girl who's far more fit than you

53

deserve."

"And how would I know that she wasn't just using me to get what she wanted?" The itching had become almost unbearable now. He raked his nails along his arm, praying it would end soon.

Vanessa drew her brows together. "You all right?"

"No, I feel like I have an army of fire ants dining on me." Sweat beaded along his forehead. If it didn't stop soon, he risked stripping off every item of clothing he had on just so he could get some relief. "The only time I've ever felt like this was the time I broke out in hives after eating shrimp."

Her eyes widened and she sucked in a breath. "I didn't know you were allergic to prawns."

He paused as Vanessa dove back into her handbag. "What are you talking about?"

"*Gamberi* is Italian for prawns. The dish she made for us—it was fried lasagna with prawns and lobster."

"Let me see your mirror." She handed it to him, and he peered at his reflection in the dim light. His lips were already swelling, and raised splotches dotted his cheeks and neck. "That vicious—"

"Don't get your knickers in a bunch. Even I didn't know you were allergic to prawns, and I've known you for years. I doubt she gave it to you on purpose." Vanessa handed him a small white pill. "Now take that before your throat swells up and you stop breathing."

He swallowed the tablet and pulled several hundred-dollar bills out of his wallet—more than enough to cover the check and leave the waiter a good tip. "I need to grab that EpiPen in my glove compartment."

"I couldn't agree more. You're getting all puffy." She laid her napkin aside and gave a wistful sigh. "It's a shame to leave all this lovely food behind."

Adam stood and loosened his collar. "I'll bring you back."

"So I guess that means you won't be closing this place down." She grinned and bounded up from her chair, locking her arm through his. "That's the best news I've heard all night."

He'd agree to anything if it meant he'd stop itching. He just prayed Vanessa was right and Lia didn't do this out of spite.

****

Lia flipped through the stack of receipts bound together by a paper clip and punched the numbers into her spreadsheet. Sales tonight had been higher than normal, but then, not every table ordered five entrees for every course like Adam and his date did.

She clenched her hand into a fist, hating every twinge of jealousy that filled her when she pictured the two of them together. It was obvious they'd been together for a long time, from the way they ate off each other's plates to the way they left arm and arm with each other. The only consolation came with the knowledge that Adam was no different than Trey, and she was better off without a two-timing bastard like him.

At least she'd proven her point to him. He'd even praised her shrimp dish in front of his date. She clicked her spreadsheet and stared at the numbers. Maybe if she offered to pay double, maybe even triple her current rent, he'd let her stay. It would mean she'd have to stay at her mother's a bit longer, but it would be worth it to keep La Arietta.

She threw the receipts on her desk and leaned back in her chair. No matter what solution she came up with, it still came back to Adam choosing her over Amadeus Schlittler. Thankfully, Dax's suggestion that she sleep with him was out of the question, especially now that she knew he already had a girlfriend. She'd been tempted to tell the stunning British woman all about Adam's behavior on the boat this weekend but had thought better of it. The last thing she needed was to cause a scene in her restaurant.

A creak came from the opposite end of the kitchen, and Lia's breath caught. Everyone else had left a good half hour ago, and she'd locked the doors behind them. She reached under her desk for the Louisville Slugger she'd kept hidden just for situations like this and peered through the cracked-open door.

A shadow moved across the dark kitchen, running into the metal workstation where the salads were made. A low grunt filled the silence.

She tightened her grip on the bat. Her office not only was the only light in the whole place, but also where the safe was located. Whoever was out there would be drawn here.

The shadow came closer. It was a man, probably an inch or two over six feet, medium build. She jotted this down to memory so she could give some description to the police in case he got away. Of course, he'd have to survive her home-run swing first.

She brought the bat up to her shoulder and waited. The door swung open, and she attacked like Sammy Sosa going after a fastball. The bat connected with the man's midsection, dropping him to his knees. She followed it up with a sharp swing up that knocked him to the ground. "That'll teach you to break into my restaurant."

But instead of some kid in a ski mask, her trespasser wore a dark suit.

The bat slipped from her hands, and a string of Italian expletives exploded from her mouth. "What the hell are you doing here?"

Adam groaned and rolled to his side, leaving a puddle of blood on the floor next to him. "Last I checked, I still owned this building. Besides, your front door was left unlocked."

A few more four-letter words flew from her lips as she stepped over him and went to fetch a napkin and a bag of ice. He'd managed to rise to a sitting position when she returned. "Let me take a look."

He shoved her off. "You've done enough damage."

She flipped the lights on and took a better look at his injuries. His nose was bleeding, and his eyes were puffy. A splotchy rash covered his face and hands. "I'll take the blame for the nose, but that's it."

He stood slowly, wincing with every inch but still refusing her help. "Your *gamberi* are responsible for the hives."

Shit! If she'd known he was allergic to shrimp, she would've never given them to him. Her desire to wow him

57

with her cooking had backfired in epic proportions.

He snatched the napkin from her hand and hobbled to one of the workstations, leaning on it while he tried to staunch the trickle of blood coming from his nostrils. "Why do you have a baseball bat in your office?"

"I'm often here alone at the end of the night. It's safer than a gun."

"Especially with a swing like yours." He pinched the bridge of his nose and hissed. "I think you broke it."

"I seriously doubt that. Now quit whining and put some ice on it." She heaved a sigh of relief when she saw his nose still maintained its perfectly straight profile. "So, back to my original question—what are you doing here?"

He pressed the ice bag to his nose, muffling his words. "I wanted to know why you gave me something with shrimp in it."

"I didn't know you were allergic to shrimp. I just thought you didn't like them, and I wanted to prove to you that I could create a dish with them that even you'd love." Her head throbbed as though she were the one who'd been on the receiving end of the bat. Instead of helping her cause, she'd made an even bigger mess of things. "I'm sorry about the hives."

He lowered the ice bag enough to reveal one bloodshot eye. "But not the aggravated assault."

Any sympathy she was beginning to feel for him ebbed as a new wave of indignation crawled up her spine. "How was I supposed to know it was you? You could've at least announced your presence or something like that. You know, a little 'Hello, I'm not a thief breaking into your restaurant to rob and rape you.' And last I checked, my name is still on the sublease, which doesn't give you permission to come and go as you please."

"Point made, even though your front door was unlocked." He adjusted the ice bag so it covered his eyes again. "If I dare come here again after hours, I'll wear protective padding."

"Oh, come on, don't tell me you didn't get a bruised up a few times growing up. I know you have six brothers."

"Yes, but I'm the oldest, which meant I was always bigger than them." He paused before adding, "At least until we got into high school."

She covered her mouth to stifle the giggle that arose when she pictured his six brothers ganging up on him. Her anger evaporated. She lowered the edge of the ice bag and met his gaze. "Next time, I promise not to swing as hard if I know it's you," she teased.

The corners of his eyes crinkled. "Not as hard, eh?"

She grinned and nodded, releasing the cold plastic bag and moving on to the mess he'd left on the floor. After sopping it up with a few paper towels, she sprayed the area with a bleach solution. "So, what did your date think of the evening?"

"Are you talking about Vanessa?"

"Was that her name?" She scrubbed the tile with renewed vigor, making sure she got every last drop of blood up.

"Vanessa is not my girlfriend."

"That's right, because you're too busy to date." *And too busy courting Amadeus Schlittler to take over my restaurant.* The paper towel she was using disintegrated into shreds.

"I am." He tossed the bag of ice into the sink. "Vanessa is an old friend of mine and a food critic for the *London Times*. She was shopping in New York earlier this week, so I flew her over tonight to see what she thought of La Arietta."

Lia froze. A food critic from London? "Did she like it?"

"The woman wouldn't stop raving about your food all the way to the airport."

The breath she'd been holding whooshed out. She sat back on her knees and let the news sink in. "Too bad we'll be forced to close at the end of next month."

"Damn it, Lia." Adam paced back and forth in front of her. "You're not going to make this easy, are you?"

"I'm not the one who brought a food critic to dinner."

He crouched down in front of her and stared at the grout between the tiles. "I find myself in a very uncomfortable situation, one where I might have to change my plans."

Her heart fluttered. "So you're going to renew my lease?"

"I didn't say that." He snapped his head up and stared at her as though that penetrating blue gaze could bend her to his will. "I still want Schlittler to open up a restaurant in one of my Chicago properties, and nothing is going to change my mind about that. However, if there's another location that meets his needs, then I'll let you stay."

"Oh, thank you!" Lia flung her arms around him, knocking him flat on his back. His breath came out in a grunt, reminding her of the injuries she'd caused. She raised herself up on her arms. "Oh, sorry."

Even though he winced, he pulled her back to him. His heart hammered under her hands. He brushed her hair out of her face and asked softly, "Are you always this rough with men?"

Every single warning bell in her body went off, telling her to back away from Adam now, but she continued to close the gap between them. "Just the ones that drive me crazy."

"Lucky me." He guided her those last few inches until their lips met. The kiss was slow, sensual, controlled. In other words, different than the ones they'd shared on the boat, but still having the same dizzying effect on her.

He broke his lips away from hers. "I hate to end this, but a kitchen floor is not very romantic."

She scrambled back, her face on fire. What was it about Adam Kelly that made her lose any bit of common sense she had? She gave him a nervous laugh. "Yes, I suppose it's a bit hard and cold."

He got up and brushed the invisible wrinkles out of his immaculate suit. "So, does La Arietta ever have a slow night?"

Back to business again. Probably for the best since she turned into a ball of raging hormones every time he touched her. "Not really. We've been booked solid every night for the last three months."

"Is there a night where you could get away from work?"

"I don't like being away from here." A smudge on the

stainless steel workstation caught her eye. She grabbed a towel and polished it away. "I worry something will slip if I don't oversee every little detail."

He started to laugh, but ended up covering his nose with his hands. "And I thought *I* was a control freak."

"La Arietta is all that I have, and I'm the one responsible for her success."

"But you need a break every now and then."

"Oh, no, no." A spatter of grease remained on the side of the stove, begging her to remove it. She sprayed the bleach solution on it and scrubbed. "If I step away for even a second, I come back to a huge mess."

Adam caught her elbow and led her away from the stove. "So there's no one here you can trust?"

The heat from his touch flowed up her arm, unknotting the muscles in her shoulder and tempting her to bury herself in his arms. She glanced back at the stove to make sure the grease was gone. "Well, maybe I could trust Julie, my sous chef, for a few hours."

"Which brings me back to my original question— which night would be the best for your getaway from here?"

Her spreadsheet popped into her mind with the daily listings of sales and profits. "I suppose Sunday would be the slowest night for business."

"Good, because I'd like to take you out then."

Her pulse stuttered. "You mean like on a date?"

He leaned his head to the side and furrowed his brows. "Well, maybe not exactly a date. Maybe more like a chance to spend some time alone with you and get to know you better."

She grinned and leaned into him. "Like a date."

"I don't have time to date."

"Neither do I." She breathed in his scent and closed her eyes. As much as she loved La Arietta, the idea of spending time alone with Adam tempted her enough to say, "Sunday sounds good to me."

"It sounds good to me, too." His voice rumbled low and hungry. He ran his fingers along her cheek, catching on her jaw and tilting her face up. For a second, he looked ready to kiss her again. Then he released her and took a step back. "I'll call you to set up the time and place."

Her stomach flip-flopped, but she couldn't tell if it was due to excitement or nerves. Maybe a combination of both.

He paused at the door leading to the darkened dining room. "By the way, I promise to announce my presence if I ever decide to visit you after hours, so please leave the bat in your office."

She laughed again, this time without the nervous edge. "I promise I'll leave it under my desk if I know it's you."

"Glad to hear that." His smile fell into something more wistful and serious. "Until Sunday, then."

Chapter Five

"I need some advice."

Adam winced as soon as he said the words. As the oldest, he'd always been the one his brothers turned to when they needed advice. Now he was on the phone with his youngest brother, trying not to sound completely pathetic.

"And you came to me?" Gideon asked. "Must be pretty bad if you're venturing this far down the totem pole."

Gideon might be barely old enough to legally drink, but he was the most like Adam when it came to temperament. Plus, it helped that his youngest brother had a reputation for leaving ladies swooning in the aisles, thanks to his films.

"I have a date Sunday night—"

"*You* have a date?" Disbelief dripped from his brother's voice. "Mister 'I'm too busy rescuing Kelly Properties from the brink of disaster to give a woman the time of day?'"

"I'm not *that* uptight," Adam countered, even though his inner voice was calling him a liar. "And the business has never teetered on the brink of disaster."

"You'd never know it from the way you're always going on about increasing expenses and decreasing revenues and a sluggish economy. Makes me happy my job is recession proof."

"Yeah, I just saw how much that movie studio is willing to pay you for walking around with your shirt off for two hours."

"Hey, I'm more than just eye-candy. It's actually a serious role for once, and I'm looking forward the challenge." Gideon quickly changed gears. "So, back to this alleged date?"

"I met this woman, and she finally agreed to go out with me—"

"Finally agreed?" Laughter filled the line. "You must've lost your touch with the ladies from spending all that time in the office if you had to work on convincing a woman to go out with you."

"Will you please let me finish without interrupting me?" Adam got up from his desk and paced along the wall of windows in his office. Downtown Chicago looked so calm and peaceful from up here, so very different from the jumble of rattled nerves that tied his stomach in knots. "I admit, I've been out of the dating game for a while, and I need some help impressing her."

"And the Kelly family name isn't impressive enough?"

"Not with her. If anything, it has me in the dog house."

Gideon let out a low whistle. "What did you do?"

"I don't want to get into it."

"You're the one who called me for advice."

Adam stopped and raked his hand through his hair.

"Okay, fine, I'll give. The timing isn't great, but the...."
The chemistry? The sparks? The way she invaded his
thoughts for days after seeing her? "The attraction is
definitely there."

"Please say she's more attractive than that peroxide and
silicone filled Barbie Caleb's been lusting over."

Those generous lips and seductive green eyes filled his
mind, and his pants grew uncomfortably tight. "Much
prettier."

"And she's attracted to an old man like you?"

If her response to his kiss was any indication, then yes.
The way she had moved against him on the kitchen floor
last night had him wanting to rip their clothes off and
finish what they started on the boat last weekend. "Pretty
sure. Thankfully, I still have a few teeth left in my mouth,
being the old man that I am."

Another laugh from Gideon. "Then why do you need
my help?"

"Because there have been some hiccups the last few
times I've been around her, and I have a feeling that after
the third strike, I'll be out. Hence, the reason why I want
to make our official first date perfect."

"Why not give her a night out on the town? Take her
to a fancy dinner and the opera or something like that."

Adam pulled out a pen and jotted down the opera idea.
At least Lia would be able to understand the lyrics, unlike
some of his previous dates. "Good, but I want to do
something more than the restaurant thing. Touchy subject
right now."

"Now I'm intrigued. What is it about this woman that

has you wanting to go above and beyond?"

Gideon's question stumped him for a moment. He sank down into his desk chair and rubbed his jaw. He'd dated plenty of women over the years, had some flings he later regretted, and even had his heart broken a few times in high school and college. But he'd never experienced the pull, the hunger, the raw need that shot through him whenever he was around Lia.

His mouth went dry as he croaked, "Let's just say I really want to see where things go with her."

"Damn, you have it bad for her. You haven't already started picking out names for your future kids or anything, have you?"

"It's just a date, not a marriage proposal. Besides, I'm not sure I want kids."

"Says the man who drives a Volvo," Gideon teased. "At least tell me her name."

What harm could come from that? "Lia."

"The one Mom bought for you at an auction?"

Enter a new level of mortification that would no doubt be followed by months of ribbing from his brothers. "That's not what happened."

"Not according to Caleb. He said you couldn't keep your hands off of her, and that Bob from the lake patrol actually stopped the next day to apologize for scaring you and the lady you had on Mom's boat."

Adam ran his finger along his collar. Great. By now, everyone along Geneva Lake probably knew about how his near hookup turned into an epic fail. "Can we please get back to helping me impress her?"

"It sounds like you two just need to go someplace private. Why not just skip the wooing and invite her over to your place?"

"That might come across as too forward."

"And what happened on the boat wasn't?"

The sounds of a scuffle followed by muffled voices cut off the conversation. Then Sarah, Gideon's assistant, entered into the discussion with her usual no-nonsense attitude. "Adam, I can't believe you're asking Romeo here for advice, so let me give you a quick tip so he can get back to the set where they've been waiting for him for the last five minutes. All women like to be indulged. If you're just looking for a quick screw, then follow your brother's advice and take her to the opera. If you're looking for something more, then try to learn more about her interests so you can share them. Does that help?"

"Maybe." Lia had said cooking was her passion. If he could show her he was interested in the same thing by making dinner for her.... "Time for a crash course in the culinary arts."

"How long do you have before this big date?"

"Sunday."

"Then I suggest you have the Food Network on twenty-four-seven." A few more hushed whispers followed before Sarah spoke again. "I'll have Gideon call you back once they're done shooting for the day."

Then the phone clicked dead.

Adam set his phone down on his desk and ran his fingers through his hair. He had one more chance with Lia, and he hoped to God he wasn't biting off more than he could chew with this idea.

****

"Got a minute?"

Lia jumped in her seat before spinning around to cover up her computer screen. She'd been so engrossed in an article on what men like during sex that she hadn't heard Julie approach her office. "Um, sure."

Julie peered around her, a half-grin playing on her lips. "'How to Drive a Man Wild in Bed', huh? I suppose that has nothing to do with why you asked me to take over the kitchen for the second Sunday in a row?"

Her cheeks burned, but she forced a smile onto her face. "Maybe."

"Let me guess—the suit called after enjoying the dinner you fixed for him and his date last night and asked you out?" Julie crossed her arms and leaned against the doorjamb.

"She wasn't his date. She was a food critic from London." Lia hit the power button on her screen before Julie could read any more. "And he stopped by last night after we closed and asked me out."

"And you're going to take a page from Dax and seduce him into letting you keep your lease?"

"Oh God, no."

"Then why were you reading advice from *Cosmo*?"

"Because...aw, shit." She slumped back in her chair. "I should've never agreed to this date because no matter what happens, there's always the lease."

"Yeah, that's the problem with mixing business with pleasure." Julie pulled up a spare dining room chair from the hallway and sat down. "Even if the date has a happy ending, he'll be wondering if you're sleeping with him to save the restaurant."

"I'd never do such a thing."

"I know that. You know that. But does he?"

It had been all too easy to surrender to his kiss last night. If they hadn't been in the kitchen, she probably would've ended up naked and fully satisfied. And who's to say she wouldn't end up that way Sunday night? "Any chance you can call in sick on Sunday so I can back out of this gracefully?"

Julie's grin widened, but she shook her head. "I'm looking forward to being in charge almost as much as you're looking forward to a night of mattress aerobics."

"Dammit." She untied her ponytail and combed her fingers through her hair, letting the mindless task calm her frazzled nerves. "Fine. I'm a grown-up. I can have dinner with Adam Kelly without letting things get out of hand. Then there's no reason for him to think I'm exchanging sex for the lease."

"Good plan." Julie rose from the chair and carried it with her. "Of course, if one thing leads to another, try nibbling on his ear. I haven't met a guy yet who didn't turn to complete goo from that. But the whole scratching your nails down his back thing? Highly overrated."

Lia waited until she was alone again before turning her computer monitor back on. Maybe she'd been reading this all wrong. Maybe all he wanted was dinner and a chat. Maybe she was the one who couldn't control her hormones around him and was jumping the gun.

But one thing was certain—she'd let Adam know she wasn't going to use sex as leverage for La Arietta.

CHAPTER SIX

"I'm not going to sleep with you to keep my restaurant," Lia said in one big whoosh before her courage left her.

Adam quirked a brow. "Glad to know we're on the same page there." He opened the door all the way and ushered her into his Lakeshore Drive condo. "Although I do think that's jumping the gun a bit, don't you?"

Shit!

The idea of turning around and running back to the elevator was sounding better and better. She lowered her gaze and came in just far enough for him to close the door behind her. "I'm sorry, Adam. It's just that when you invited me over to you place, the first thing that came to mind was—"

"That I'd try to force you into my bed by using your restaurant as leverage?" He lingered by the door, his hand still on the handle. His mouth pressed into a firm line. "I see I've already made a favorable impression on you."

"No, it's not that, it's just—" She threw her hands up into the air. "I don't know what I was thinking. I mean, if I just thought you were after sex, I wouldn't have agreed to have dinner with you in the first place, but I—"

A sizzle from the kitchen stopped her verbal diarrhea. She sniffed the air and caught the scents of smoky cumin and singed black pepper. "You're cooking dinner?"

"Oh, shit, it's burning." Adam dashed past her into the kitchen and flipped the flank steak cooking on the indoor grill. He poked it with his tongs. "Do you think it'll be okay?"

She came up beside him and inspected the meat. Whatever rub he'd used looked a bit charred, but everything underneath it looked fine. "I think it's still edible."

"They had this Bobby Flay marathon on the Food Network yesterday, and somehow, I got the impression I could turn into a super chef from watching it."

She laughed and took the tongs from him, moving the steak to the edge of the grill where the heat was less intense. "Have you ever cooked anything before?"

"Just Easy Mac." He snatched the tongs back with a boyish grin, bumping her aside with his hip. "I'm a man. Grilling dead animals is part of my DNA."

"Then don't let me get between you and all that secret information encoded on your Y-chromosome," she said, still laughing, the awkward start to the evening now a distant memory. "So why did you decide to take on the grill when we could've easily gone out to dinner?"

"Would trying to impress you be explanation enough?" He nudged the steak with the tongs, not looking up from it. "I just thought it would be nice for you to have someone cook for you for a change."

A warm glow ignited near her heart and quickly spread through her chest. "That's very sweet of you." She glanced around at the scattered ingredients on the counter. "And ambitious."

"Did you miss the memo where I always get what I want?"

Her grin mirrored his. If this was the only side to Adam she knew, falling for him would be a no-brainer. He was smart, funny, sexy as hell—all things that would have any woman tripping over her high heels to grab him like a Black Friday special. If only she could forget the fact that he held the future of La Arietta in his hands.

"Is there anything I can do to help?" She started cleaning up the food scraps on the counter.

He left the grill and coaxed her away from the mess. "Yes, you can pick out a bottle of wine to go with dinner."

"And what's on the menu this evening?" she asked, even though she had a good idea based on the scraps of cilantro and parsley she'd just cleaned up.

"Grilled flank steak with chimichurri sauce, roasted vegetables, and mashed potatoes."

"Sounds delicious." She surveyed the kitchen and saw that the oven was on, and a pot with steam coming out from under its lid simmered away on the stove. Everything looked to be under control. "Where's the wine?"

He pointed to the glass cabinet by a large wooden table in the next room. "Get whatever you'd like."

Lia's jaw dropped as she inspected the contents of the wine cabinet. Adam had excellent taste in wine. Expensive, but still very good. She settled on an Argentinean Malbec and opened it in the kitchen. It tasted like black cherries, followed by hints of black pepper toward the end. "Perfect."

Adam took a sip from the glass she offered him and nodded in approval. "Good choice."

"I'd like to think I know a thing or two about pairing wine with dinner." She eased onto the barstool on the opposite side of the grill. "Everything smells delicious."

He gave her smile that only hinted of his usual confidence. "Thank you. Dinner will be ready in a few minutes. Why don't you take a look around?"

A dismissal from his realm, but one she easily understood. She always got nervous when someone was peering over shoulder while she cooked.

Adam's high-rise condo had an open feel to it with the kitchen, living room, and dining room all flowing into each other. A small balcony overlooked the lake, and the traffic along Lakeshore Drive below winked like stars. The floor was covered with light-toned wood, a sharp contrast to the cherry cabinets in the kitchen and the dark brown sofas in the living room. The decor was a cross between modern and masculine. Elegant, but still relaxed enough that she could imagine Adam and his brothers watching the Bears on the sixty-inch flat screen TV.

In other words, perfect for a well-to-do bachelor.

She ran her fingers across the buttery-soft leather sofa and realized with a start that she could be comfortable here. *Get your head on straight, Lia. He invited you for dinner, not to move in with him.*

The scent of something burning wafted into the living

room. Lia turned around to see black smoke billowing out from the pot on the stove.

Adam cursed and pulled it off the eye with his bare hands, hissing and shaking his fingers a second later.

"Run them under some cold water." Lia grabbed the pot holders and lifted the lid. The stomach-turning odor of scorched potatoes filled the kitchen. "The water boiled off," she explained as she carried the pot over to the sink.

"Damn it." His shoulders slumped as he stared at the disaster in the pot. "So much for trying to impress you."

She rested her head on his shoulder. "It's not a complete loss. We still have the steak and the veggies, right?"

"Yeah, I suppose so." He shook the water from his hands, which thankfully were not blistered. "I had it all strategically planned so everything would be ready at the same time."

"The first rule about cooking is that nothing ever goes according to plan." She stuck the pan under the faucet and peered at the vegetables roasting in the oven. "Do you have any cornmeal?"

"If I do, it'll be in the pantry." He pointed to the tall, narrow cabinet at the end of the kitchen.

After a minute of digging, she found what she was looking for. "Where are your pans?"

"By the stove." He wandered back to the grill, watching her the whole time. "What are you doing?"

"I'm going to make some polenta."

****

Fifteen minutes later, Adam's momentary pity party

had vanished. He unwrapped the flank steak from the foil Lia had instructed him to place it in and divided it into two portions. "Steak's ready."

Lia brought over two plates with deep orange mush on them. "The roasted red pepper polenta is ready, too. Now, just place the steak on top like so and then add the chimichurri."

While he did that, she pulled the dish with roasted peppers, onions, mushrooms, and carrots out of the oven. The aroma made his mouth water. *At least I didn't mess that up.*

She dished up the veggies and stood back with a grin. "*Voilà!* Dinner is ready."

It wasn't the way Bobby Flay had presented the meal, but it still looked nice. He carried the plates to the table. "And now we feast."

Lia followed with the wine and poured them each a glass before sitting next to him. "Thank you for cooking."

"Don't thank me until you try it." But the first bite drove away any doubts that lingered. The steak was tender and moist, and the polenta Lia had made complemented the spices and the chimichurri perfectly. "Not bad."

She nodded in agreement as she chewed. "Not bad at all. Want to come work for me?"

He laughed and reached for his wine. "Beginner's luck."

"Still, it's a fantastic start."

He paused with the glass still at his lips. Despite the setback with the burning potatoes, his plan to make a good impression on a first date with her had gone far better than he imagined. "Thank you. That means a lot coming from you."

Her eyes appeared to be a softer green than before, more like new spring grass rather than emeralds. She held his gaze over the rim of her glass as she took a sip, and all thoughts of the meal before him vanished. There were far more tempting things to taste—like her lips. But then he remembered the first words out of her mouth when she arrived, and pushed those thoughts out of his mind. As much as he wanted her, he didn't want to cross that line unless she initiated it.

He cut into his steak while she asked him questions about what it was like to grow up in a house with six brothers. He answered them, sharing stories of some of his exploits and earning a few chuckles as a reward. But it wasn't until their plates were almost clean that he realized the entire conversation had revolved around him. He hadn't learned a single thing about Lia, but there was still time to rectify the situation.

"You mentioned last week that you didn't always want to be a chef. What did you do before?"

She choked on her wine and covered her mouth with her napkin, making him wish he could take his question back. Lia cleared her throat. "I, um, have a degree in business."

Not what he would have expected at first, but the more he thought about her success with La Arietta, the more sense it made. "From where?"

She rolled a carrot across her plate with her fork. "From Harvard."

It was then he realized he'd only begun to scratch the surface of the mysterious and complicated Lia Mantovani. "And that led you into cooking how?"

She poked her polenta, scooping up a bite before laying her fork on her plate. "I really don't want to bore you with—"

"I said I wanted to get to know you better, remember? That's the reason I wanted to have dinner with you, not because I was hoping to get you in the sack."

His words had the effect he wanted, and a few chinks appeared in her armor. "My dad died when I young, so Ma always had to work two jobs to support us and make sure I went to a good school, had decent clothes on my back, setting aside a little money for college. You know?"

He nodded, fearing that if he said anything, she'd lock back up inside.

"So when I was looking at careers, I decided getting an MBA would a good choice to have a solid future and maybe pay her back for all she sacrificed for me. I worked hard, got into Harvard's MBA program, graduated with honors."

Her story slammed to an end, and when she didn't continue, he said softly, "Go on."

"I met a man when I was at Harvard. George Augustus Hamilton, III, also known as Trey. One of those guys born with a silver spoon in his mouth who never had to work hard for anything." She didn't look at him as she spoke, but the tips of his ears still grew warm. "We got engaged right before we graduated and bought a little house in Connecticut."

Her voice cracked, and she ran her finger along the stem of her wine glass. "Trey was old money, you see, and he wanted me to be like his mom and sisters. A society wife. And I was stupid enough to think that sort of life would satisfy me. So, I stayed at home and did volunteer work and had lunch with the ladies down the street while he worked at a trading firm in Manhattan."

He didn't need to hear how the story turned out. He already heard the pain behind her words.

"A few weeks before we were supposed to get married, I learned the truth. He wanted to keep me in my gilded cage while he had his flings in the city." Her fingers curled up into her palm. "After that, I swore no one would ever keep me from doing what I wanted to do. I sold my engagement ring and used to the money to go to Italy. That's where I discovered my true passion."

She raised her eyes to him, the fear and uncertainty shining from their jade depths. Now he understood why she clung so desperately to her restaurant.

And he was the son of a bitch threatening to take it all away from her.

Adam laid his fork down, his stomach too tied in knots to enjoy the meal. "I hope Amadeus finds one of my other properties suitable."

"So do I." She reached over and covered his hand with her own. "I know I've put you in an awkward situation, and I appreciate the fact you're trying to work out a solution that meets both our needs."

If she'd been any other woman, he would've expected her to play a sympathy card to get her way, but there was nothing fake or manipulative about Lia. And he respected that.

He flipped her hand over and examined her palm. There were calluses and scars from burns she must have sustained in the kitchen, but they matched her character perfectly. Lia was someone who'd worked hard to get where she was, so different from the spoiled little rich girls he'd known his entire life. And maybe that explained part of his attraction toward her.

He laced his fingers through hers. "He was a fool to treat you that way, to not realize what a treasure you really are."

Her lips parted, the lower one trembling ever so slightly. "Thank you," she whispered before unraveling her hand from his and picking her fork back up.

****

Lia didn't know what else to say. For the last four years, she'd thrown herself entirely into her work, ignoring the one event that had started her journey to find herself. And then, just like that, she spilled her guts to Adam, a man she barely knew, and told him things only her mother had been privy to. Oddly enough, though, she trusted him.

But as soon as one burden had been lifted from her shoulders, a new one strapped itself to her. She hadn't expected him to react the way he did. For those few blissful moments while he held her hand, she forgot about the restaurant, Trey, and everything else that had been keeping her up at night. Her body relaxed from the warmth that spread through her. However, when he called her a treasure, her heart jumped, and that gentle warmth turned into uncomfortable heat that made her breath quicken and her body long to have him touch her in other ways.

No doubt about it—she was in over her head when it came to Adam Kelly.

Lia glanced down at what little was left on her plate, her appetite for food had vanished. Their brief moment of intimacy had now become awkward, a signal that she probably needed to leave. She took both plates without asking if he was done and cut a straight path to the kitchen. "I'll get started on the dishes."

The rushing water from the sink soothed her rattled nerves. There was peace here within her domain. The kitchen had been her place of refuge whenever she was troubled, and menial tasks like washing dishes or chopping vegetables had always allowed her mind to drift far away from her worries.

Until now.

Adam came up behind her and shut the water off. He pulled her hands from the soap suds. "I can do the dishes later."

She let him turn her toward him, staring at the way he cradled her wet hands as though they were delicate and precious to him. Her pulse doubled, and a fine tremor worked its way into her bottom lip.

"I said something that made you uncomfortable, and I'm sorry," he said as he brought her hands to his chest, cupping his hands around them.

"No, it's not that. I'm just feeling a little...." *Confused? Uncertain? Frightened to acknowledge that I could be falling for you?*

"Overwhelmed."

"That was the last thing on my mind, Lia." His breath bathed her forehead as he spoke, drawing her closer and closer to him. "I only wanted to express my admiration."

She took the final step to close the space between them. Her body melted into his embrace, her hands still over his heart. Time faded as she breathed his scent in and out, still unable to come to terms with her conflicted emotions. Her mind cautioned that she'd only get hurt by him, that he was no different than Trey.

But with every breath, those thoughts grew further and further away. She found a new peace in the solid lines of his body, from the firm touch of his hands as he ran them along her back, from the steady beating of his heart. This could easily become her new home.

"As much as I'm enjoying this, I'm going to have to let you go soon." He tilted her chin up, the hunger in his eyes barely contained as pressed his lips against her forehead. He ran his thumb along her lips, sending shivers deep into the lowest recess of her stomach. "I'm just a man, after all, and you are a very beautiful, very tempting woman."

He was holding back on her, restraining the desire he obviously felt for her.

The warning bells went off in her mind again, telling her to back away slowly while she still could, but her body refused to listen. She wanted Adam. She needed to feel his lips on her once again, to have him worship her as the treasure he thought she was. Yes, it would be considered crossing the line, but she'd rather enjoy one night in his arms than kick herself for letting fear hold her back.

Keeping her body still pressed against his, she reached up and lowered his lips to hers.

CHAPTER SEVEN

Adam sucked in a sharp breath, his muscles tensing as she kissed him. A needle of doubt pierced Lia's mind. Had she misread him? Had she gone too far?

Then a moan of defeat came out when he exhaled, and his resistance faded. His tongue swooped into her mouth, intertwining with hers in a seductive dance. His hands were everywhere—her hair, her back, her hips. When they finally settled on her ass, he pressed her against the hard evidence of his desire.

I should stop now before I get hurt.

Easier said than done as his kisses grew deeper, hungrier, so very much like her own. The increasing pressure of his hands against her buttocks begged her to give him permission to take the next to step. Before she knew what was happening, she had jumped into his arms and wrapped her legs around his waist. By the time they'd reached his bedroom, she'd removed both his shirt and her own. They fell back on his bed, her lips never breaking contact with his as the insatiable need consumed her.

Her bra flew off in a matter of seconds, followed by her pants and underwear. The rough denim of his jeans rubbed against the tender skin of her inner thighs, tormenting her in more than one way. She blindly reached for the button, the zipper, anything she could to free him from the confines of his clothing.

He tore his lips away from her and rose to his hands and knees, his chest billowing as he stared at her. "Oh, God, Lia, you're so beautiful," he said in a hoarse whisper before blazing a new trail of kisses along her throat down to her breasts.

He caught one of her nipples between his teeth. Her hips bucked from the exquisite sensation, moving in time with every nibble, every suck, every flick of his tongue. His weight settled over her, controlling her movements until the need welling inside broke free with a howl of frustration. "No more, please, Adam."

His head jerked up. "You want me to stop?" he asked, even though everything about him begged her to let him continue.

"No, I just want you in me now before something interrupts us this time."

He chuckled before kissing the tip of her nose. "Don't worry, Lia. I have every intention of making sure you leave here extremely satisfied."

"Prove it." She caught his face between her palms, keeping his lips occupied while she shimmied his jeans down with her toes.

He chuckled again as he removed his boxers, kicking them off with his jeans somewhere near the foot of the bed.

His cock, now free, brushed against the outer edges of

her sex. The corners of her eyes burned from the intense desire coiling within her. She'd never wanted, never needed a man this badly. Her hips protested against his weight now, frantically trying to break free and find the perfect angle where he'd fill her.

Adam reached out and whacked his hand against the nightstand. The sound startled her for only a moment before her body resumed its rhythmic undulations that broadcasted how she was more than ready for him.

"Wait," Adam said in a low groan. A drawer slid out, followed by the crinkle of a foil wrapper. He lifted his body from hers to roll the condom onto his fully erect cock. "Now we can continue."

As soon as the words left his mouth, he slid into her with such force, her heart stuttered. Four years of celibacy had taken its toll on her body. His cock stretched her walls with a burning pleasure-pain that stole her breath away. She dug her fingers into his shoulders and waited for it to pass.

"Sorry." Adam remained still, gently placing tiny kisses on her cheeks. "I'll try to be more gentle."

But as quickly as the pain hit her, it faded, leaving behind a void that demanded fulfillment. "Don't be," she gasped.

Despite her plea, he moved slowly at first, drawing out each stroke while his mouth kept hers occupied. Back and forth he went, his hips positioned at the perfect angle to hit the sensitive place inside. Her toes curled from the delightful friction. Her breath hitched in anticipation for the next thrust. Her hips rose in time to take him deeper and deeper.

As the minutes went on, his tempo quickened. A place deep within her tightened, throbbed, seized control of her. Incoherent words tumbled from her mouth. The only thing she recognized was his name. Over and over, she murmured it, begging him to continue, to take her over the edge.

"Please, Lia." His voice was tight, pained as he pleaded with her. "Please come for me."

She frantically tried to hold on to him, to keep from tumbling blindly over the cliff she was on, but her efforts were futile. She was already lost. She closed her eyes and tightened her arms around him, sucking a final breath before surrendering to the explosion inside.

****

Adam gritted his teeth and tried to fight off the increasing pressure that started in his balls and had worked its way up to the head of his cock. He had no idea what Lia's Italian mutterings meant, but he assumed she was close to coming. He quickened his pace, so desperately wanting her to experience the same bliss he knew awaited him.

Seconds after he asked her to come, her body tensed. Her thighs squeezed around his waist, her hips rising off the bed. Her fingers dug into his back. She gulped for air, fighting him, refusing to give in until she finally snapped.

Her cry of pleasure signaled that he'd achieved his goal. Her sex clenched around him, tightening and releasing with an intense ferocity he couldn't resist. With one final thrust, he surrendered. Heated ecstasy rushed through his veins, more potent than the finest cognac, drowning him in waves of pleasure. And yet, he still kept his hips pumping, still kept moving inside her, still wanting the sensations to last as long as possible.

Finally, it became too much. He collapsed, his body shaking and spent. Lia trembled beneath him. Her murmurings, distant at first, became clearer as his mind came back down from its post-orgasm high. He propped himself up on his elbows and found himself laughing.

Lia's eyes widened. "What's so funny?" she asked.

"I suppose I need to take an Italian class if I want to understand what you're saying when you come." He rolled off the bed to dispose of the condom, trying to ignore the jealous thoughts of her saying those same words to some past lover. He wanted those words, whatever they meant, to be for him and him alone.

"I—" she began before ending with a heavy sigh. "Ever since I moved to Italy, my brain has been hard-wired to think in Italian. I even dream in it."

He crawled back into the bed, pulling the covers up over them, and lay on his side. "Whatever you were saying, it was damn sexy."

She rolled over and grinned, bunching the covers up over her breasts in an unexpected display of shyness. "I suppose I just lost control of myself."

"Don't ever apologize for that." He smoothed her hair back off her forehead and placed a kiss there. "At least, not in the bedroom."

Her shoulders relaxed, but her smile faded as she watched him, growing more sober. "I meant what I said when I first arrived here tonight."

He flashed back to her rushed declaration that she refused to sleep with him to keep her restaurant. His hand stilled. Why would she be bringing that up now? The events of the night fast-forwarded through his mind, pausing at the moment where he cautioned her that he would have to let go of her soon. He'd wanted her to know that as much as he desired her, he wasn't going to push the issue of taking things to the next level.

No, she'd been the one to initiate things. She'd been the one who'd kissed him, even after he'd warned her that he wouldn't be able to refuse her if she did. And now she was the one reminding him that what they'd just shared could have ulterior motives.

He searched her face for any signs of manipulation, any self-congratulatory smirks. Instead, he saw only fear and uncertainty. His doubts eased. Whatever had prompted her to make the first move, it wasn't an act of guile. "I know," he said at last.

The corners of her full mouth rose. "Thank you."

"No, I should be the one thanking you." His body still hummed with pleasure. His eyes feasted on the beautiful woman in his bed. He had to be the luckiest son of a bitch in the world right now.

"You sound like you didn't expect us to end up here." She wiggled closer to him, giving him a sultry glance through her lashes that matched the flirtatious tone in her voice. "I thought you always got what you wanted."

"I think this was the first time I was worried about it," he teased back.

He ran his finger along her jaw, his confidence faltering by the time he reached her chin. A strange pressure filled his chest as he looked into those deep green eyes. He could fall in love with Lia right now if he wasn't careful, and mixing business with pleasure could be dangerous. Very dangerous.

She bit her bottom lip as though she could see the turmoil raging inside him. It was a delicate game they were playing, one that involved both their heads and their hearts, and they'd just placed all their chips on the table.

The ring of a cell phone shattered the silence. Lia jumped back, pulling the covers up over her shoulders. Adam closed his eyes, praying it wasn't what he thought it was.

The familiar chords of "Bad to the Bone" rocked through his bedroom once again, and Adam cursed under his breath. That was Frank's ringtone, and Frank only called for one reason.

"Sorry, but I have to take this." He slipped his jeans on and waited until he was in the living room before fishing his cell out of his pocket and answering, "This had better be important, Frank."

"Would I bother you if it wasn't?" his younger brother asked. "I'm in a bit of a bind, and I sure could use your help."

Adam sank down on the couch and pressed his palm against his temple. What had started out as a dream evening was quickly turning into a nightmare. "What did you do this time?"

The sixth of the seven Kelly boys, Frank was the only

one who'd inherited their grandmother's red hair and Irish temper to match. Of course, that also meant he could turn on the Irish charm when he wanted, like now. "I was just at a club, minding my own business, when these two guys came up to me and started giving me a hard time for flirting with one of the girls."

Adam groaned. He'd heard this story more times than he cared to count. "And let me guess—one thing led to another, right?"

"Hey, they started it." A defensive growl rose into Frank's voice. He'd made a career of funneling his rage into tearing through offensive lines and throwing quarterbacks to the turf, but unfortunately, Frank had the nasty habit of carrying his aggression off the field.

"How much damage did you cause this time?"

His brother paused. "Um, it's a little more complicated this time."

Shit! "What happened?"

Another pause. This couldn't be good. "I need you to bail me out."

Adam leapt to his feet with another four-letter word. "Why are you in jail?"

"They're trying to book me for assault, but it was all self-defense."

He paced the length of the room, mentally calculating how much Frank would cost him this time. Bail, an attorney, damages. His brother would probably need some serious PR work to clean up his image, too, if this had already leaked to the press. "You need to think before you throw a punch, Frank, or no team will want to have you on their roster."

"Bullshit, Adam. I made the Pro Bowl as a rookie. Besides, you're going to get me out of this mess, right? So nothing to worry about."

Adam curled his hand up into a fist. What he wouldn't give to be able to reach through the phone and shake some sense into his brother. "Do you have the name of any bail bondsmen in Atlanta?"

"I figured you could find one for me." Frank's voice lowered to a whisper. "And please hurry. I don't like the way some of these guys are looking at me, if you know what I mean."

"I have half a mind to let you stay there until after your hearing."

"Oh, come on, Adam. You wouldn't let your little brother get sexually violated by these perverts, would you?"

"I don't know—would it keep you out of trouble in the future?"

"I'm telling you, I'm innocent. Swear to God."

Innocent was never a word he'd associate with Frank.

The bedroom door creaked, stopping him from giving his brother the tongue lashing he deserved. Lia appeared in the doorway, fully dressed.

"I'll take care of you in a bit," he said, never taking his eyes off her. How much had she overheard?

"Why? Don't tell me you have a hot chick over or anything like that. I know you, Mr. Too Busy to Bang Something with Tits."

He wanted to tell Frank to shut the fuck up, but Lia's

presence made him watch his tongue. "I'll talk to you later," he said, fighting to keep his voice calm, and ended the call.

He threw his phone on the couch and went to her. "Sorry about that, Lia. I—"

She shushed him by covering his mouth with her fingers. "No need to apologize. I understand."

He lowered her hand, keeping it wrapped in his own. "Do you?"

"Yes."

"This is not the way I wanted the night to end."

She gave him a wistful smile. "Me, neither, but it sounds like your brother needs you, and I need to get some rest before going back to the restaurant tomorrow."

He made a mental reminder to make sure Amadeus Schlittler saw every possible property tomorrow before showing him Lia's space. "Do you need a ride?"

She shook her head. "I'll be fine." She crossed the room and picked up his phone, pressing it in his hands. "Take care of your brother, and don't worry about me."

He caught her as she tried to turn around and pulled her into his arms. He only meant to give her a simple kiss goodbye, but he quickly found himself wanting to take her right back to bed.

Lia pushed on his chest, ending the kiss at last. She backed away from him with a playful smile that let him know she'd gladly continue some other time. When the door closed behind her, a chill crept under his skin that rattled his core. She was gone, and he was already missing her.

He glanced down at his phone, cursing his brother for ruining what could possibly have been the best night in his life. But as he started looking up phone numbers on the internet, he also realized it was probably a good thing Lia had left when she did. He was getting too emotionally involved in this deal, and until he figured out what he was going to do with Schlittler, he needed to keep his head on straight and his heart locked away.

CHAPTER EIGHT

Lia twirled as she entered the kitchen at La Arietta. Everything was going to be all right. Amadeus Schlittler would open his restaurant someplace else, and then she and Adam could look forward to many more nights in each other's arms once all this was done. It was the best of both worlds.

"Somebody's in a good mood this morning, I see," Julie said with a wink. "I take it you had fun last night?"

"Fun, my cute little tight ass," Dax said from behind her, pushing her toward the office and closing the door behind Julie when she followed them. "She's practically glowing, which means only one thing—the girl got laid."

"Dax!" Her cheeks flamed, and she looked longingly at the door that was blocked by her maître d' and sous chef.

"Oh, come on. Don't deny it." He wagged his eyebrows. "And don't leave out any juicy details, either."

"Okay, that's going a bit too far." Julie shoved Dax back but didn't move toward the door. "But things did go well, right?"

They weren't going to let her go until she spilled her guts like a teenager at a slumber party. "Fine. Yes, I had a good time with Adam, but that's all you're going to get from me."

Dax exchanged glances with Julie. "Oh, yeah, she went all the way. Pay up, girlfriend."

Julie grumbled as she reached into her pocket and pulled out a twenty-dollar bill.

Lia's mouth fell open. "You two made a bet over whether or not I'd sleep with him?"

"You betcha." Dax snapped the bill open several times to get any wrinkles out. "Julie thought you'd hold out until you knew he wasn't going to kick you out, but I got a good view of Mr. Hottie, and I knew you wouldn't be able to resist him once he put the moves on you."

She tried to come up with some harsh retort, but words failed her. Her face was probably as red as a tomato. She pushed her way past them, finding her voice again once she stepped into the domain where she ruled without question—the kitchen. "You two stop speculating about my personal life and get to work. We have an hour before we open for lunch, and I don't want to hear any excuses."

They both scurried back to their workstations—Julie to the pasta machine and Dax back out into the dining room.

Lia hid inside the walk-in fridge and let the cool air bathe her flushed cheeks while she looked to see what she could use for today's special. Their teasing had struck a nerve in her. As much as she had enjoyed her evening with Adam last night, there would always be that lingering doubt in her mind that one of them had subconsciously seduced the other to get their way.

I just have to trust Adam to keep his word.

Her mind said she could, but her heart was still too wary to trust any man completely. After all, she'd trusted Trey, and look where that had gotten her.

She emerged from the fridge with several bunches of asparagus in her hands, already mentally forming a list of the other ingredients she needed to make the vegetable the centerpiece of a risotto.

It was one second past opening when Dax burst into the kitchen. "Lia, you need to come out here *now*," he whispered.

She followed hot on his heels into the dining room and stopped short. A man who looked like Rutger Hauer after a *Queer Eye* makeover stood by the maître d' stand, his arms crossed as he stroked his chin. "No, I'm definitely certain," he said in a strong Austrian accent, "this all has to go. Every bit of it. Ick!" He squeezed his shoulder blades together as though he'd just dunked his fingers into slime.

Mr. Bates wrote something down on a notepad and nodded. "Yes, Mr. Schlittler. Shall we proceed to the next room?"

Amadeus Schlittler strutted into the dining room the way supermodels did on the catwalk, swaying hips included. "Oh, God, this is simply horrendous. It all has to go, too. The rustic look is simply passé. I want the black marble to continue into here, and mirrors along this wall to reflect the city lights."

Lia's teeth clenched. She started counting to ten before she lost her cool, making it all the way to eight before she reached them. "Is there something I can help you with,

Mr. Bates?"

Before he could answer, Amadeus barged in. "This is none of your concern, little girl. Go back into the kitchen and keep scrubbing pots."

Her blood pressure skyrocketed, her pulse pounding along her scalp. "I am the owner and executive chef of La Arietta, and I demand to know what you are doing here."

Amadeus rolled his eyes and did his best Valley Girl sigh. "Mr. Bates, will you please deal with her? I don't have much time to decide what I want to do with this place, and I'd rather focus my creative energies on something other than this speed bump." He spun around on his heel and rocked one the chairs at a nearby table, wrinkling his nose.

Mr. Bates cleared his throat. "Ms. Mantovani, as you know, Mr. Kelly still plans to lease this space to Mr. Schlittler once your lease is done, so we're here—"

"No, you have it all wrong," she interrupted, shaking her head as though this was all a bad dream. "Adam said he'd be showing Mr. Schlittler other properties."

"What's this about other properties?" Amadeus rushed back to them. "Mr. Kelly and I had an agreement. I want this space and nothing less. I *deserve* this place."

Lia was thankful she'd left her knives in the kitchen. She curled her hands up into fists, her arms pressed against her sides to keep from knocking the other chef's teeth out. "And what makes you think I don't deserve to stay here?"

"Oh, please," he replied with a dismissive wave of his hand. "You're just a little nobody. I'm Amadeus Schlittler, one of the greatest culinary geniuses of all time. My restaurants have more stars than you'll ever dream of seeing in your life. Why should Mr. Kelly keep you when he can have me?"

The insults hit her like a slap in face. Why would Adam let her keep this place when he could have Schlittler? And now that he'd gotten what he wanted from her in the bedroom, why should he keep his word to convince the diva-chef to open his restaurant elsewhere?

Her eyes burned, but she refused to show any signs of the weakness trembling inside her. She lifted her chin and said in a cold voice, "Perhaps so, Mr. Schlittler, but until the end of the month, it's my name on that lease, so get your self-absorbed ass out of my restaurant."

Schlittler's eyes widened as though she was the first person who'd ever spoken to him that way. Then they narrowed into a sneer. "For now. Enjoy it while you can, little girl, because on the first of the month, this will all be mine."

He snapped his fingers and turned around. "Come along, Mr. Bates. I can continue to give you all my demands on the way back to Mr. Kelly's office."

Lia kept her muscles locked into place, staring at the entrance long after they left. She didn't crumble until Dax laid a hand on her shoulder. "Oh, sweetie."

Fat, scalding tears rolled down her cheeks and plopped onto her crisp, white cotton chef's jacket. She'd been a fool to ever believe Adam. He always got what he wanted, and this was no exception. And she'd been stupid enough to fall for his bullshit. A treasure? Ha!

Julie pressed a glass into her hand and wrapped an arm around her shoulders. Dax stood guard in front of them as they hurried back into the safe confines of her office. "Have a sip of grappa and get it out of your system," her sous chef urged.

But it wasn't as simple as that. She'd been tricked into believing Adam had actually cared for her when all the while, he was plotting on destroying her business to make way for that conceited piece of strudel. She'd opened her heart to him, and he'd betrayed her in a far worse way than Trey ever had. He'd given her hope and then squashed it.

It was over now. Lia set the glass on her desk and let the first in a series of silent sobs rack her body.

****

Adam bolted up in bed, his heart hammering as he stared at the numbers on his alarm clock. 4:17 PM. A glance at the late afternoon sun outside his window only confirmed that the display was correct.

He ran into the bathroom to check his reflection and frowned at the stubble shadowing his cheeks. He might be able to bypass a shower to save on time, but there was no way he could leave the house without shaving. He snatched the razor from its charger and began running it over his cheeks while he grabbed a fresh suit from his closet.

Cheeks now smooth, he turned his phone over to speaker and dialed Bates's number. "Yes, Mr. Kelly?"

"Please tell me you showed Mr. Schlittler some of my other properties," Adam said as he hopped into his pants.

"No, sir. I thought you'd decided the Michigan Avenue property would be the best location for him."

Adam cursed and shoved his arm into a clean shirt. "That was last week. I wanted to show a few other places before that one."

"I'm sorry, sir, but if you don't tell me these things, how am I to know what to do?"

He'd gotten halfway down his shirt when he realized he'd buttoned it wrong. "I know. It's my fault—I was planning on taking Schlittler there myself and personally trying to convince him they were suitable locations."

"Ah, I see. That explains why Ms. Mantovani seemed so surprised to see us today."

Adam froze, his hammering pulse threatening to choke him. *Shit, shit, shit!* "Please tell me you didn't take Schlittler to La Arietta today."

"Since you were not available this morning, I decided to show Mr. Schlittler the property before he became more, um, impatient."

He sank down onto the bed, his mind paralyzed. He'd been in bad situations before but nothing of this magnitude. If he'd had any hope of having a relationship with Lia, he could pretty much kiss it goodbye now. She'd probably never want to speak to him again, much less trust him.

"Mr. Kelly, are you still there?"

"Yes, Bates, I'm just trying to figure out the best way to smooth this all out." He ran his fingers through his hair. "It's my fault for not showing up this morning. I was up late taking care of some personal business, and I must have slept through my alarm."

"A pity, sir."

He stood up and walked the length of his bed, his hands clasped behind his back. "Schlittler is still in town?"

"Until tomorrow morning, sir. He's staying at the Waldorf Astoria. I made reservations for him to dine at Alinea tonight at eight."

Adam thanked his lucky stars to have an assistant like Bates. "Please call Alinea and make sure they have room for me to join him. I'll try to sell him on some of the highlights of the other properties and convince him to take a look at them next week."

"Very good, sir. As for Ms. Mantovani?"

He jerked to a stop. Lia was a far trickier situation. "I'll deal with her later tonight after I've spoken to Schlittler." *Because if I can't convince him to look at other places, then I'll have to deliver the bad news to her in person.*

"Thank you, sir." The relief on Bates's voice only added to his unease. Whatever had happened this morning between Lia and Schlittler was probably much worse than he'd first let on. "I'll call Alinea now."

Adam sat back down on the edge of the bed, his tie looped through his fingers. In less than twenty-four hours, everything that had been going well in his life had suddenly come crashing down around him. He stood at a crossroads. Last night had cemented his feelings for Lia, but would he be able to tell her no when it came to business?

Chapter Nine

The numbers on the screen blurred together. No matter how hard Lia tried to focus on them, her tears kept threatening to spill over. Somehow, she'd managed to get her shit together long enough to get through the work day. But now that she was alone in her office, the anguish of Adam's betrayal seized control of her thoughts over and over again.

You should have just used sex as a bargaining chip.

She shook that renegade thought from her mind and wiped her eyes with the back of her hand. As much as she wanted to keep her restaurant, she refused to lose her integrity. She'd slept with Adam last night because she was attracted to him. Too bad he was planning to screw her over in more than one way.

And yet, he'd seemed so sincere when it came to trying to get his brother out of whatever trouble he'd gotten into.

Lia stopped typing and rested her face in her hands. No matter how much she wanted to paint him as a villain, she couldn't. Too many little details like that gave her a glimpse of the complicated mess that was Adam Kelly. Ruthless businessman, yet caring brother and son.

And let's not forget damn good lover. Trey had never made her come that hard in all the years they were together.

A whimper of defeat rose into her throat. She should've never accepted his invitation for dinner as long as the future of her career hung in the balance.

"Hello, Lia?" a man called from the dining room.

Speak of the devil. She eyed the baseball bat under her desk. Could she get away with pretending she didn't hear him?

A loud crash filled the darkened kitchen, preventing her from using that excuse. She reached along the wall outside her office and turned on the lights. "Just for your future reference, the light switch is right by the door. You know, in case you want to come and harass Schlittler in the middle of the night like you do me."

Then she slammed her office door closed. If he wanted to pester her, she'd given him more than enough warning.

Of course, Adam always got what he wanted, and tonight was no exception. He didn't even bother to knock before opening the door. "Lia, we need to talk."

She continued to punch in the numbers from the receipts in her hand, albeit a bit harder than required. "Schlittler already came by this morning to dictate his plans for the décor, so you can spare yourself that conversation."

"So I heard, and I apologize for that."

"Apologize?" She turned to face him, her earlier tears replaced by barely contained fury. "I think it might be a little late for that."

He crossed his arms and leaned against the doorframe, blocking her escape. "An apology is never too late, especially when there's a big misunderstanding."

"Yes, there was a big misunderstanding." She shoved him out of her way and started picking up the stack of metal bowls he'd scattered on the floor when he came in. "I misunderstood you when you said you'd be trying to convince Schlittler to open his restaurant elsewhere."

He took the bowls from her hand and held her in front of him, his warm hands on her upper arms. He didn't need to use force—his touch alone weakened her defenses and turned her legs into goo. His lips pressed into a thin line "So all you care about is your restaurant? Is that it?"

The accusation in his voice stung. "You can call me whatever you want, Adam, but I'm not a whore. I meant what I said last night. I just didn't expect you to pull this so quickly after getting what you wanted from me." She shrugged free from him and continued cleaning the kitchen.

"If you think I just made you some glib promises to get you in my bed, then explain to me why I felt the need to spend the last four hours trying to convince Schlittler to look at other properties next week."

She froze, unsure if she should trust her ears. "Guilt?" she squeaked.

"Damn it, Lia, you have me so wound up, I feel like I'm stuck on one of those hamster wheels—always running, but getting nowhere." He loosened his tie and slipped it out from his collar. "I overslept this morning, and I forgot to tell Bates about my plan. He should have never brought Schlittler here."

"But he did." Her chin quivered at the memory of the chef's harsh words.

"And that's why I came here to apologize. Bates informed me that he was beyond rude." Adam leaned over a container left out on the dessert station, peeling back the plastic wrap and sniffing. "Is this the same raspberry sauce you made last week?"

Lia cursed under her breath. "I can't trust anyone here to put things away properly." She took the container from him, the cool metal easing her worries that it had been left out too long.

Adam halted her and took it back. "I was just going to use this."

"To do what?"

"This." He stuck his finger into the sauce.

Her heart hammered at how he'd just ruined the entire batch, but her reprimand never left her mouth once Adam smeared the sauce along the fullest part of her bottom lip. He leaned forward and kissed her, gently sucking the sauce off before he pulled away.

"Delicious," he murmured before repeating the actions again. "Of course, you're sweet enough without the raspberry sauce."

Don't fall for his games. Don't let yourself be seduced by his— She sucked in a sharp breath as he moved to dabbing the sauce on her ear lobe and nibbling it off. "This isn't going to work."

He answered her feeble protest with a mere "uh-huh" before continuing to drag his sauce-covered finger along her neck, followed quickly by the flat of his tongue.

A tingle of pleasure rushed from her head to the deepest part of her gut. She didn't resist him when he backed her against the metal table where all the desserts were plated. She didn't stop him as he removed her thick white chef's jacket and threw it across the kitchen. And she didn't cry out in protest when he continued to smear the raspberry sauce on her exposed skin and remove it with a wickedly sensuous combination of licks and nibbles.

Adam had worked the straps of her tank top down past her shoulders before he paused. His thumb brushed across her breast, and he gave her a mischievous grin. "Do you want me to stop?"

She shook her head, already knowing what was lying in store for her if his fingers were telling the truth. "I'll have to throw the sauce away now anyway."

"Then I'll use as much as I need." Just as she'd expected, he lowered her top to expose her breast and rubbed the bright pink sauce on it.

What she didn't expect him to do was lift her up on the table just as he was taking her nipple into his mouth. The cold, hard metal contrasted with the hot, velvety texture of his tongue as it swirled around the aching peak. She moaned and arched her back, melting into him. When he reached the point where pain mingled with pleasure, he moved to the other breast and repeated the same dizzying choreography of licks and nips that left her tense and wanting by the time he finished.

In any other situation, the idea of having sex in her kitchen would've horrified her, but Adam had her ready to strip her clothes and any remaining shreds of control she had left. She wanted him even more than she had last night. She needed him.

The throbbing in her sex intensified as he removed her pants and underwear with one quick tug. The raspberry sauce ended up on her ankles, her knees, her thighs, inching ever closer to the part of her body that demanded release.

And Adam knew it. The closer he got to her sex, the slower and more deliberate his motions became. What had once been a streak of pink sauce an inch or two in length now travelled the entire length of her thigh. What had once been a quick stroke of his tongue or a playful nibble had turned into a long, drawn-out lick that set her flesh on fire. She whimpered and said his name in a plea to stop teasing her.

At long last, he knelt in front of her and draped her legs over his shoulders. His breath tickled her slick flesh as he whispered, "So beautiful, and so delicious."

The cool raspberry sauce did little to ease her burning desire, but thankfully, his tongue found its way to where she needed him most. It flicked across the exquisitely sensitive skin of her clit, sending bolts of pleasure shooting straight to her toes. Her muscles tightened, growing more and more tense as he brought her closer to the edge, only to back away as he changed the tempo of his tongue. It moved away from the tiny nub and delved into her sex with long, languid strokes.

Adam repeated this game over and over, taking less and less time between the two dances. She threaded her fingers through his hair, holding him close to her, begging him not to stop until she finally shattered. She fell back onto the table, her hips rising against his mouth. His tongue continued to spiral along her flesh with each pulsating wave of her orgasm, drawing it out until she was left breathless and sated.

She had no idea how long she lay on the table, but the cold metal reminded her she was naked. Adam wrapped his arms around her and helped her up, holding her against his chest and stroking her hair while her pulse returned to normal. Minutes passed before she realized he was still fully clothed. "Aren't you going to finish?"

"I would love to," he replied, pressing the hard bulge in his pants against her, "but I don't happen to have a condom available at the moment. I don't suppose you do?"

She shook her head, a wave of shyness overcoming her. She pulled away and crossed her arms over her chest. "No, I'm not the sort of girl who imagines she'll be having sex in her kitchen."

"Yes, there's that pesky problem of mixing business with pleasure." He dipped his finger in the sauce one more time and swiped it on her swollen mouth. "In this case, I'm more than willing to make an exception, though."

She let him kiss her one more time, wondering what rule he was willing to make an exception on. She got her answer when he ended the kiss and said in a gravelly voice, "I'd better stop before things get out of hand. I wouldn't want you to think I was seducing you so you'd forget about what happened today."

"I thought it was an apology." She waited until hope lit up his eyes before giving him a slow, easy smile. "And in this case, I think I can find it in my heart to forgive this misunderstanding."

"And for that, I'm extremely grateful." He buried his face against her neck, placing a trail of kisses along her skin until he came to her ear. "Of course, I'd be even more grateful if you'd come home with me tonight so we can finish this in more comfortable surroundings."

Her body was already saying, *Yes, yes, yes*, but she hesitated in order to weigh the consequences of her answer. The more time she spent in Adam's arms, the more entangled her heart became. Would she still feel the same about him if she lost her restaurant? Or was she just setting herself up to be hurt in the end?

She searched his face, seeing less and less of the cold-hearted businessman who'd come into her restaurant last week with news that he wouldn't be renewing her lease. Instead, she saw the man who made her heart race and her body yearn.

The man she was quickly falling for.

She ran her fingers along his cheek and took a deep breath. She'd have to trust him with the things she treasured the most and pray she chose wisely.

"Let's go back to your place.

CHAPTER TEN

"It's not like you to back down on a proposal, sir." Bates handed Adam a folder. Inside, a single sheet of paper listed the cost analysis of his original plan versus his new idea. He'd have to shoulder the loss, but if that was what it would take to sell it to his investors, he'd do it.

Adam snapped the folder shut and continued down the hallway to the boardroom. Shadowy figures moved behind the frosted glass windows like unseen enemies. His pulse kicked up a notch. He was going into battle in a way he'd never done before. Usually, he went in trying to sell his investors on an idea he was passionate about. Now, he was asking them to go along with a new plan after he'd gotten them to sign on to the old one. He didn't know if it would be better to act humble or continue with his usual air of confidence. Either way, he'd eventually have to admit he'd made a mistake, and that made the muscles along his back twitch.

Bates cleared his throat. "By the way, did you see that lovely feature La Arietta got in the *London Times* this weekend?"

"No, I haven't."

"You should read it, Mr. Kelly. Miss Kingsley had nothing but praise for Ms. Mantovani's skill. I took the liberty of printing it out for you." He pointed to the folder.

Adam grinned and thanked his lucky stars his father had hired Bates years ago. That article would be one more tool in his arsenal as he went into battle, and if it helped, Bates was in for one hell of a bonus.

His assistant stopped several steps short of the boardroom's entrance. "I wish you luck, sir."

"Thank you, Bates." *I'm going to need it.*

Adam adjusted his tie, smoothed his jacket, and steeled his nerves. In a little over two weeks, he'd made a complete one-eighty about his decision on which restaurant would be best for the Magnificent Mile property. Now he needed to make sure the others saw it his way.

He opened the door and strode into the boardroom with his head held high. "Good afternoon, gentlemen. Thank you for coming today."

"We're glad to have a chance to speak with you," Raymond Vilowski, a member of the Chicago City Council and a longtime business partner, replied, "especially after hearing the disturbing news Mr. Schlittler has been sharing with us."

Adam glanced across the room and found himself staring to the cold blue eyes of Amadeus Schlittler.

Shit!

"Hello, Mr. Kelly," the chef said with a ripple of his fingers. "I hope you don't mind my presence today. After all, you're here to discuss the location of my restaurant, the one you've convinced all these men to invest their money in, right?"

Adam's jaw tightened, holding back every expletive he'd wanted to hurl at Schlittler over the last week. Instead, Adam held his gaze as he sat at the head of the table. "No, I don't mind at all," he said in an even voice.

"Marvelous." Schlittler rose from his chair and circled the men at the table with slow, long steps like a sovereign deciding how to deal with a band of traitors he'd just captured. "As I was telling you, Mr. Kelly enticed me with the prospect of opening my latest restaurant on the top floor of his building on Michigan Avenue. Naturally, I expect only the best, and even though that property barely lived up to my expectations, he then tried to convince me to consider several...." He paused, rubbing his fingers together as though he'd just touched something covered with filth. "...less desirable locations."

The men all turned to Adam, their eyes asking why. But it was Ray who finally gave them words. "I thought you had this all laid out, Adam. You said you'd be evicting the current tenant when the lease was up, making way for Chef Amadeus."

"That was my original intention, but it seems the current tenant, Chef Lia Mantovani, has been making quite a name for herself lately." He opened his folder and found the article Bates had so cleverly inserted for him. "Just this week, she got rave reviews from a food critic at the *London Times*."

He handed the article to Ray first, followed by the

feature in *Food and Wine* talking about how Lia was one of the hottest new chefs in America. He waited as the pieces of paper circulated the room. Schlittler pretended to buff his nails on his sweater while the men read them, his expression of annoyance speaking volumes even though he remained silent.

The articles had almost made it back to Adam when Ray spoke. "That's all well and good, but she's not the same caliber as Chef Amadeus."

"Thank you, Mr. Vilowski." Schlittler gave Adam an "I-told-you-so" smirk.

"Perhaps not yet, but she is local talent." A few of the men nodded, and Adam saw the table slowly turning in his favor. "That got me to thinking—why should we destroy what she's built in less than a year to make way for an outsider? Chicago's always had a proud Italian heritage, and she's taking it to the next level."

"Adam brings up a good point, Ray," Thomas Blakely said from the opposite side of the table. As one of his father's oldest friends, Tom had more than once served as the voice of reason when the Kelly family was deciding where to place their money. "In an economy where small businesses are suffering, there's more pressure from the voting public to have the government's support and nurture local businesses."

Ray shifted in his chair. "But as Adam pointed out when he got us to sign on to this venture, the appeal of Chef Amadeus's restaurant would help all the businesses in the building."

"Perhaps, but you're up for re-election next year, right?

How do you think your opponents would use the fact that you were willing to force a local girl out of business in favor of a foreigner?" Tom propped his elbows on the table and clasped his hands together loosely while he waited for Ray to respond to his question.

Ray took on the challenge and leaned forward, mirroring Tom's stance. "I'm not the only person at this table, though."

"Ray's correct," Adam said, hoping to swing the momentum of the conversation back in his direction. "All of you have agreed to invest money into Mr. Schlittler's restaurant, and if he decides to pull out at the last minute, I wouldn't hold any of you responsible for the previously signed contracts."

"But why are you making him move?" Ray asked. "Why not relocate La Arietta? Then you can have the best of both worlds."

"If I make La Arietta move, that would be a considerable expense, both for Chef Lia and for us. Not to mention, it would require her to close the restaurant for the time it took her to move everything." Adam leaned back in his chair, hoping the move would encourage the others to see this as a closed argument. "I've spent the last two days showing Mr. Schlittler every upscale commercial property I own, including the one in Lincoln Park, and he refuses to consider any of them."

Now all the heads turned to the chef, who rolled his eyes. "Apparently you have a different definition for upscale here in Chicago. I am Beverly Hills. I am Fifth Avenue. I am not Lincoln Park."

"You're also Las Vegas Strip last I checked, so don't go throwing around all the locations of your other restaurants in an effort to impress us." Adam drummed his fingers on the arm of his chair. "You want to be where the money is, and I'm more than willing to put you there."

"Just not willing to let me have the location you promised me."

"What it sounds like to me is that Adam made a bunch of promises that he's now trying to back out of." Ray pushed back from the table. "If that's the case, I need to remind you that we *all* signed that agreement to encourage Chef Amadeus to open his restaurant in the Michigan Avenue building."

Adam nodded. "I understand, Ray, but I also wanted to let you know what I've discovered in this process and ask all of you to consider my new proposal."

"The time for this information you're presenting should have been before you promised Chef Amadeus that location, not after." Ray stood and looked to the other men. "I don't know anything about this Chef Lia what's-her-name and frankly, I don't care. When we have someone of Chef Amadeus's caliber available, my money's going with him."

He turned to Adam. "I'll give you until Friday to decide what you really want."

"Finally, someone who speaks sense." Schlittler walked around the table and looped his arm around Ray's. "Let's go and talk about some of the menu items I'm creating for my Chicago restaurant. The others will follow."

They walked out of the boardroom, leaving Adam and

the three other investors in silence. "Do you all feel the same way?" he asked.

Tom pressed his fingers against the tip of his nose as he looked up at the ceiling. The other two men stared at their laps. After a minute, Tom said, "You've brought up a few things to think about, Adam."

"I know, but I didn't want to keep plowing into this headfirst once I unearthed this information."

"About Chef Lia?"

"And about Chef Schlittler." Now that the arrogant prick was gone, Adam could at least speak openly about him. "As you can see, he's very demanding and difficult to work with. As big a name as he is, I'm beginning to wonder if he'll also become a big problem."

"Meaning?" one of the other men asked.

"I'll e-mail you the list of demands he's already given us as far as the Michigan Avenue property is concerned. I foresee more demands like this in the future, meaning we'd have to continue to finance them. Men like Amadeus Schlittler don't come cheaply."

The other men nodded.

"It seems Ray has already set a deadline for us," Tom said, "so I'm willing to wait until then to see if we can come up with the best solution."

"And as I said before, I won't hold you to your contracts if I decide it's in the best interests of the company not to give Schlittler the Michigan Avenue property." Adam stood and shook the hands of the other men. "Thank you again for coming. I'll get you that information later today, and I encourage you to see the gem that we already have in place."

The other men left, but Tom remained in his chair. Age may have lined his face and turned his hair white, but it had only sharpened the intelligence in the older man's eyes. "I have the sneaking suspicion you're leaving something out, Adam."

Adam fetched the papers and put them in his folder, ignoring the trickle of unease that slid down his spine. "I told you everything that's pertinent from a business perspective."

"But you left out the personal perspective."

"I don't know what you're talking about."

"Come now, Adam, I've been friends with your parents since before you were a twinkle in their eyes, and Maureen was telling me all about how she introduced you to Lia a few weekends ago up at the lake house."

"I'm glad she did. If she hadn't, I wouldn't have discovered what a fabulous chef she is." Or what a passionate lover she was, either. Lia had spent three nights of the last week in his arms, making the nights she wasn't with him a form of agony that grew harder to bear with each passing day. Traces of her scent covered his pillowcase. Memories of her laughter echoed through his empty living room. And the peace he knew lying beside her, completely spent after making her cry out his name in ecstasy, called to him throughout the day. She was slowly turning his condo into a place he couldn't wait to come home to, but only if she was there to greet him when he did.

Tom watched him but said nothing. The old man

probably saw right through him, but at least he had the decency not to say anything more about it. "We need to have dinner once your mother gets back from Vancouver," he said as he stood.

"I agree." His mother had left this morning to take care of his brother after Ben had suffered a season-ending knee injury two days ago. "The surgery was today, so she should be home in a week or two." He stood and shook Tom's hand. "Thank you for being the voice of reason."

"Don't thank me yet. Ray could hold you to the original contract. He's got enough fingers in the town's pie to make life difficult for you and Lia."

"I know." He just prayed it wouldn't come to that. He wanted both Lia's and Schlittler's restaurants—the question was, which one did he want more?

"So here's a little piece of advice from me. Remember Robert Cully?"

Adam nodded, wondering where this conversation was going. His father had hired the private investigator several times over the last decade, usually to gather information on suspected fraud cases. He glanced down at the files, then back up to Tom. "Is there anything you think I should hire him for?"

"You don't make it far in Chicago politics without getting your hands dirty along the way." He winked and walked out of the boardroom, giving Adam the spark of hope he needed to see himself out of this mess.

CHAPTER ELEVEN

Lia hummed an aria from one of Verdi's operas as she tossed some tortellini in a warm gorgonzola sauce with prosciutto and peas. The last entrée of the night was about to go out to the dining room, bringing her one step closer to the end of the evening. She'd given her mother the same line about staying late at work once again—meaning *don't wait up for me*—so she could stop by Adam's tonight. It was easier than trying to explain that she was sleeping with someone she'd known less than a month.

Of course, if La Arietta was forced to close at the end of the month, she'd have to come up with a different excuse.

That is, if she continued to see Adam.

As much as she enjoyed his company, things definitely were more complicated now that they'd become lovers. They never mentioned the lease when they were together, but it was never far from her mind when she left his arms. She kept her heart guarded, afraid their relationship would end once she no longer had her restaurant. But every night in his bed only made it that much harder to leave when the sun came up. She was happy with him, miserable without him, and constantly on edge when it neared the time to see him again.

Dax came into the kitchen. "I had to keep Mr. Hottie in a Suit from barging in here like he owned the place."

"He does own the place," Lia replied with a laugh. "But thank you. He's usually not here during business hours."

"Meaning he's been here after hours, I presume?" Dax tailed along behind her as she went out into the dining room. "Stopping by for dessert?"

Heat rolled into Lia's face like a line of thunderstorms. "That's none of your business."

Adam stood by the maître d' stand, waiting for her with a smile that remained polite but with an underlying gaze that already spoke of the naughty things he wanted to do with her. He rocked back and forth on his feet with his hands clenched in his pockets.

"Told you she'd come for you, Mr. Kelly." Dax took his position behind the stand and gave her a saucy wink.

Thankfully, no one was around to hear the innuendo in his voice. Lia grabbed Adam's arm and led him to the corner by the elevators. "You're a bit early tonight."

"I had to see you."

Her pulse quickened. Perhaps he had some good news about the lease. "What about?"

Adam opened his mouth but snapped it shut as a pair of guests left the restaurant and pushed the button for the elevator. "Is there some place we can talk in private?"

"There's my office."

"Someplace else?" The heat in his eyes told her talking was the last thing on his mind.

Her sex clenched at the thought of what was lying in store for her this evening, and her breath quickened. "Can this wait until after we close?"

He shook his head and pulled her into the stairwell. They ran down three flights, stopping only long enough for Adam to punch in a key code and unlock the door that led to a darkened hallway full of empty offices.

As soon as the door closed behind them, his lips were on hers, hungry and demanding. Any cry of protest she made faded into a moan of pleasure. He pushed her against the wall, his body pressed against hers while he tugged at her clothes. "I need you now, Lia."

****

I'm like a junkie craving my next hit.

Or at least, that's the closet thing Adam could think of as he fumbled with the zipper of his pants. He'd gone home after the meeting and tried to come up with a solution that would please everyone, but every time his mind circled back to Lia, a new wave of longing consumed him.

She'd only been in his condo four times, but she'd already left her mark there. The half-empty bottle of wine in the kitchen. The extra crumpled napkin left on the dining room table. The magazine on the coffee table left open to an article about a Napa Valley winery. The indention in the pillow next to his that smelled faintly of the peach-scented lotion she kept on the table beside his bed. All little reminders that made him miss her.

He'd gone to the restaurant with the intention of inviting her back to his place to watch a movie and unwind before going to bed, perhaps even to broach the subject of possibly relocating her restaurant in case Schlittler and Ray refused to back down. But by the time he got there, something else had seized control of him, a burning thirst for her that had to be quenched before he lost all control. A basic need that now had him kissing her like a starving man while he slipped her panties down around an ass that fit perfectly in his hands.

She moaned and shimmied against him, the motion both freeing her from her underwear while rubbing her against his already aching cock. Sparks of teeth-gritting pain shot up his spine. If he didn't get inside her soon....

"Wait," she said, pushing him back. "We don't have a condom."

He reached into his wallet and pulled out the one he'd tucked in there a few mornings ago. "I've learned to be prepared when it comes to you."

Relief softened the tension in her face. She grabbed him by his shirt and pulled him back to her, assuming control of the kisses with a passion that left him breathless. She wanted him as much as he wanted her, and he set a new record for donning the proper attire for the occasion.

All it took was the subtle prompt of cupping her ass to have her jump into his arms and wrap her legs around his waist. He wasted no time sliding into that hot, slick place that fit him so perfectly. A sigh of contentment filled the empty hallway, but he had no idea if it came from him or her.

Sometime during all the commotion, she'd managed to

slip his jacket off, leaving him only in his dress shirt as he pumped his hips back and forth, slamming his cock into her over and over again like a madman. Every stroke was pure bliss. Every cry of passion that came from her lips was sweeter than any music he'd ever heard. Every rake of her nails along his back drove him forward like a coachman's whip.

"More, Adam, more." Lia writhed against the wall, her eyes half-closed, her breath coming as quickly as his. Her body tightened around him, from her arms and legs to the tight walls of her sex.

His own body tightened in response, his balls rising, increasing the pressure building at the base of his shaft. He fought to hold it back, to make sure she enjoyed the same explosion of pleasure he knew was lying ahead of him, despite the frenzied nature of their fucking. "Oh, God, Lia, I can't, I can't—"

The words died in his mouth as a feral growl took their place. He plunged into her one final time before surrendering to his orgasm. But that last stroke was all she needed to join him over the edge. Her higher pitched scream joined his, her sex tightening and releasing in perfect rhythm with the waves of release rolling through his cock. His legs wobbled from the intensity of it all, and they slid down the wall together.

Minutes passed as his pulse drummed through his body like a marching band doing a victory celebration. Sweat beaded along the nape of his neck, dampening his hair where her fingers twirled through the strands. He sucked in a deep breath that was scented with peaches, sex, and another note that was undeniably Lia.

"I—" she began before breaking off into a nervous giggle. "I've never done anything like that."

He lifted his head from where is rested against her hair and pressed his forehead against hers. "Neither have I."

His confession bought another giggle from her, less nervous this time. "It's always been one of my little fantasies, but it was far better than I could've ever imagined."

She took the words right out of his mouth. He pulled her closer to him, tucking her head under his chin. "I hope you'll forgive me for being so blunt. I'm finding that I'm having a hard time controlling my desire for you."

"I would have stopped you if I didn't feel the same way."

What strange twist of fate had brought her into his life this way? Oh, wait, his mother. But for once, perhaps his mother knew what she was doing by forcing them to meet each other.

A blast of cold air from the vent above reminded him that they were sitting in the middle of a hallway without their pants. He kissed the top of her head and loosened his arms around her. "Perhaps we should get dressed."

She nodded, her bottom lip jutting out ever so slightly. "I suppose you're right. I have to start closing."

"Maybe I should hang around until you've finished." His cock twitched to life, already growing hard at the idea of making love to her again. "We can go back to my place when you're done."

She laughed and ran her finger along his shaft. "At the

rate we're going, you'll be ready to go again by the time we reach the staircase. And then I'd be all distracted because all I'd be thinking about would be when I can have you inside me again."

He remained where he was as she got up and put on her underwear and pants. Something in her words troubled him. Their sexual chemistry was undeniable. But was there anything more between them? Did they have enough in common outside the bedroom to turn this from a fling into a long-term relationship?

The night he cooked her dinner came to mind as he pulled his pants back on. Yes, they'd been able to chat, to enjoy each other's company before things eventually turned to the bedroom. And as much as he enjoyed getting twisted in the sheets with her, he now found himself craving something different.

"Lia, would you like to meet me for lunch tomorrow?"

She froze like he'd just asked her to jump into Lake Michigan in the middle of a blizzard. "You mean like this?"

"No, I mean like you and me, fully clothed, enjoying a meal together."

Her lips parted for a few seconds, her expression wistful, before the practical edge returned to her voice. "As much as I'd love to join you, I can't. I have to tend to my own lunch crowd here."

"Can't you play hooky for a day?" He pulled her back into his arms, placing several light kisses along her face. "It's just for a few hours, and I promise to have you back in plenty of time to prep for dinner."

She gave him a half-hearted shove, followed by a laugh when he continued to plant small pecks on her cheeks. "You don't give up until you get what you want, do you?"

"Now you know why I always get what I want."

"Fine, but that means I can't come home with you tonight. I have to get everything ready for lunch without me."

"I'll make that sacrifice." Besides, he'd already scratched his itch moments before and cleared the lust haze from his mind. "Can you meet me at eleven?"

"Where?"

It only took him a split second to come up with the one place he knew he'd be able to keep his hands off of her. "My mother's house in Highland Park."

CHAPTER TWELVE

Lia double-checked the address Adam had given her. Yep, this was the right house. Or mansion, to be more precise. When her mother had told her a few weeks ago that the lake house was more a cabin compared to Maureen Kelly's Highland Park home, she hadn't been kidding. A lead weight dropped to her stomach as she came up the circular driveway, her palms sweating on the steering wheel.

By the time she rang the doorbell, her hands refused to stay still. She checked her appearance in the glass in case she'd missed some small smear of her lipstick or piece of lint on her shirt. Adam and his family were part of the Chicago elite, no matter how much they downplayed it, and she was out of her realm.

She braced for a slobbering mound of white fur when the door opened, but saw only Adam. "Where's Jasper?"

"Don't worry about him. I took care of that problem." He took her hand and led her inside, pausing only to press a quick kiss on her lips. "It's just you and me today."

Her stomach began to unwind as she gazed up the massive carved cherry-wood staircase. "Your mother isn't here?"

"No, she's in Vancouver taking care of my brother, Ben."

Her hands finally stilled. Even in this mansion, she could still find solace in the fact that she didn't have to put on airs in front of anyone else. "Which one is he?"

"Come here and I'll show you."

He led her into a room off to the side. Tiffany glass inserts framed the massive windows overlooking the bright blooms of the garden and immaculate green lawn beyond it. A pair of well-cushioned Queen Anne wing chairs stood on either side of a fireplace big enough for her to crawl into. A square table made of dark, heavy wood with a brown leather insert stood off to the side with two decks of cards inviting someone to play with them. All and all, the décor reminded her of Adam's place—expensive and elegant, but comfortable and inviting.

Picture frames lined the mantle, all dwarfed by the family portrait that presided over the wall above. A man who looked very much like Adam sat next to a 1980s version of Maureen, surrounded by seven boys. The youngest son appeared to have been only a few months old when the picture was taken. She swallowed a giggle when she noticed the two lines of silver tracks running along Adam's teeth.

He caught her looking at the picture and gave a half-cough. "Yeah, I keep telling Mom it's time to update the family photo—perhaps something where I'm not wearing braces—but she won't listen to me." He held up one the smaller frames. "This was taken last Christmas."

A line of seven men grinned back at her, their arms all thrown around each other's shoulders. Their hair color varied from black to bright red, and their height varied within six inches of each other. Their eyes were all blue, even though two of them had eyes that were more of a slate blue rather than the bright, piercing blue of Adam's eyes. But they all had the same smiles, the same chin, the same crinkles around their eyes. In other words, there was no denying they were brothers.

Her heart squeezed a little tighter as she looked at the picture. She'd never had a brother or a sister growing up and had always wanted to be part of a large family. It was only when she moved to Italy and was taken in by her cousins that she got her wish.

Adam ran his finger along the line, starting with man next to him. "That's Ben, Caleb, Dan, Ethan, Frank, and Gideon."

Each of the Kelly brothers now had a name and a face for her, although a couple of the men she hadn't met seemed vaguely familiar. "What do they all do?"

"Ben's a goalie for Vancouver—or at least he was until he tore his knee up last week. It ended his season, but he seems to think it's the end of his career." His face grew serious, his lips pressing into a straight line. "I'm waiting for his pain meds to wear off before I try to talk some sense into him." His mood lightened as he added, "That is, if Mom hasn't already.

"Caleb, whom you met at the lake house, is a pilot in the Air Force. Dan's finishing up his surgery residency.

Ethan," he said, pointing to the man with straight black hair that came down to his shoulders, with hints of tattoos peeking out from under his clothes, "is in a band."

She took the frame and studied him closer. "Isn't he the lead singer of Ravinia's Rejects?"

Adam nodded as through it were some local garage band instead of the multi-platinum rock group known around the world. He continued down the photo, pointing to the man with red hair who seemed to be made of pure muscle. "Frank is a linebacker for Atlanta, and Gideon is an actor."

She recognized the youngest brother as one of the hottest leading men right now, and it had almost as much to do with his acting abilities as it did with his status as of one the sexiest men in Hollywood.

Her fingers fell from the frame. Every single one of them had done something extraordinary, making her feel more insignificant with each passing second. "You have quite an accomplished family. Your mother must be very proud."

He shrugged and placed the frame back on the mantle. "Our parents always encouraged us to do what we were passionate about. I suppose you of all people should know how powerful it can be to work day to day in what you love the most."

"Yes, I do." She'd been cautious not to bring up the lease over the last two weeks, but it was times like this when it weighed on her like a two-hundred-pound barbell. Part of her wanted to mention that she'd love to keep working with her passion, but it meant she'd have to ask him about his decision to let her keep the restaurant. As it was, she'd already started scouting out places that were in her price range, but none of them even came close to what she had now.

She turned back to the picture, staring at Ben. "Don't be too hard on your brother when you talk to him. I can understand how disheartening it is to be faced with the prospect of not doing what you love."

Adam met her gaze for a moment, then looked away. "Would you like to see the rest of the house?"

"Is this an upstairs tour or a downstairs tour?"

He jerked to a stop, his hand on the doorframe leading to the hallway. "Excuse me?"

Her mother had always warned her to bite her tongue. This was one the times she'd wished she'd followed that advice. "I know how things get when we're alone together, and since we've already checked off the 'hurried sex in a place where someone might walk in on us' fantasy, I was asking if you'd invited me here to check off the 'having sex in your parents' bed' fantasy or whatever it was you had in mind."

He approached her slowly, one brow raised. "No, it's the exact opposite."

She didn't realize she'd been holding her breath until it whooshed out.

"Unlike most teenagers, having sex in any place where my parents could catch me was never a fantasy of mine. Even though I know my mom's all the way in Vancouver, I still worry she may walk in on me, so sex is the last thing on my mind at the moment." He stopped and threaded his fingers through hers. "I invited you here for the very reason I gave you last night. The two of us, fully clothed, enjoying a meal together."

The warmth of his hand flowed up her arm and settled into her chest, chasing away her doubts. "I'd like that."

"Me, too. I even packed a picnic lunch." He led her into the cavernous white kitchen that perfectly suited the Victorian feel of the home. "It's such a nice day out, I thought we could enjoy the sunshine"

"That sounds wonderful." She couldn't remember the last time she'd been able to stretch out under the sun and let it beat down on her skin. The spring day was warm enough to be comfortable, but the light breeze kept things from getting too hot.

Adam grabbed the basket and blanket sitting on one of the counters and motioned for her follow him outside. They wove along the winding path that cut through the garden. The air was full of the sweet scent of roses and gardenias, their fragrant blooms nodding as they passed. It was an ideal place to have a picnic, but Adam continued on to the soft grass ahead, finally stopping under the branches of an oak tree that must have been planted when the house was built.

"This look good to you?" he asked, spreading out the blanket.

She nodded and sat down beside the basket. "What's on the menu?"

"I bet you enjoy asking that for a change," he said with a laugh. "We have a gourmet selection of sandwiches." He pulled them out one by one. "Turkey and Gouda. Ham and Swiss. Roast beef and cheddar. And last, but not least, the classic PB and J."

It was times like this when she forgot that he was a successful businessman who was probably worth millions. Adam may have been born to money, but he also acted like a common Joe when he was out of the suit. "What? No caviar and champagne?"

"Nope, but I have potato chips, dill pickles, and the ever-refreshing Coca-Cola." He held out a bottle of pop like it was a bottle of Dom Pérignon.

She couldn't suppress a grin. "Impressive."

"I learned my lesson when it came to cooking." He popped the lid off the bottle and handed it to her. "Keep it simple."

"Simple is good from time to time." She picked up the turkey sandwich and unwrapped the deli paper around it. "Besides, it still took some time and planning to pull this together."

"Yep, complete with a trip down to the local supermarket." He pulled out a pink box and a book. "For dessert, we have cupcakes and poetry."

"Now I know you went all out." She picked up the book and read the spine. "John Donne?"

"One of my favorite poets. I developed an appreciation for him while I was at Oxford."

"And when was that?" she asked before taking a bite of her sandwich.

"In college. That's where I met Vanessa, the woman I brought to La Arietta."

The food stuck in her throat as she tried to swallow,

and the unwelcome sensation of jealousy prickled along the base of her spine. "Oh?"

"Yeah, she lived in my building. Don't let her posh accent fool you—she's the daughter of a mechanic and a school teacher—but she's been a good friend over the years." He opened the book and pulled out a piece of paper. "In fact, she wrote this about your restaurant."

The first thing she noticed was "*The Times*." The next thing she realized as she scanned over the review was that Vanessa had raved about the food. "This is fabulous."

She wanted to sound excited, but her voice sounded hollow. What good was this review if she was forced to close her doors in a little over a week?

Adam must have heard her hesitation because he lowered the paper enough to meet her gaze. "I told you I would do my best to let you keep your restaurant, and I'm working on it."

A dozen questions flashed through her mind. What was he doing? Had he shown Schlittler any of the other places? What did the chef think of them? When could she expect to have an answer? But she pressed her lips firmly together, asking none of them. She'd already made one verbal faux pas today. She didn't need to insult Adam again.

Those blue eyes of his never wavered as he watched her. "You want to say something. I know it."

"Yes, but I'll keep it to myself."

"One of the things about you that impresses me is the fact you're more than considerate about keeping our business out of our pleasure. Most women I know have no problem pressing their own agendas when they're with me, but you've remained relatively silent."

She laid the review down, soaking in the praise a second longer before replying. "You know how I feel about it. I don't need to make a pest of myself. Besides, I do enjoy your company, all business aside."

"I've never doubted that for a moment." He cupped her face in his hands and placed a chaste kiss on her lips, pulling back a fraction of inch when he finished, so that their noses still touched. "You've placed me in an awkward position, you know."

She brought her hands up to his arms. "I'm sorry, Adam."

"No, don't apologize." He pulled back and played with his chips, not eating them. "Before I met you, I knew what I wanted and I had no problem staying on course until I got it. But with you...." His brows bunched together and rubbed his hands on his jeans. "I'm learning the hard way that compromise doesn't come easy."

Her pulse quickened. "Then why did you stray off course this time?"

"I thought that was obvious." He leveled his gaze on her, the heat in his blue eyes enough to leave her feeling hot and bothered and entirely over-dressed. "I've seen how much you enjoy your passion, Lia, and if I could only grasp ten percent of that passion, I'd be a very happy man."

A new kind of warmth flooded through her, one that overwhelmed the heat of desire and left her far more content than even the most powerful orgasm. The fact that he cared enough about her to change his plans so she could be happy made her heart flop as clumsily as her tongue for a several beats. And although it seemed too small of a reply, she managed to say thank you.

"Don't thank me just yet. I still have a few more things to take care of before I can safely say the lease is yours, but I'm working on it." He picked up the book and lay back, bunching a corner of the blanket up into a makeshift pillow. "Shall I entertain you with some of Donne's sonnets?"

She curled up next to him, placing her head on his chest. The position had almost become second nature to her now, a place to call home while in his arms. She'd worried about the possibility of falling in love with Adam, but now there was no denying the fact. With each passing day, he won more and more of her heart and left her more and more vulnerable to having it broken. But for now, she'd savor every moment she had with him.

The steady drum of his pulse beat in time with the rhythm of the words he read aloud. "Go and catch a falling star...."

****

Adam paused after he finished reading "The Triple Fool" and looked down at Lia. She'd fallen asleep beside him, her dark lashes casting deep shadows on her cheek. The sunlight that filtered through the leaves above shimmered in her hair like liquid gold. He ran his fingers through the silky strands, committing every sensation to memory.

His father had told him years ago to find a woman he

could enjoy the quiet moments with. At first, he'd laughed at the idea. But as he grew older, he began to see the wisdom behind his father's advice. He'd been in relationships where the sex was awesome, but that was it. Then there were the relationships where awkward silence would take over, a sure signal that it was time to end things. He'd never been with a woman where he was absolutely content to watch her sleep, until now. This was what he wanted this afternoon—confirmation that he could enjoy the quiet moments with Lia.

He closed his eyes and tried to imagine a future with her, one where she was the last face he saw every night and the first one he saw every morning. It was all too easy to visualize. He could stand behind her every night as she cooked, his arms around her waist so he could swing along with the rhythm of her hips as she swayed in time with her spoon. She'd let him sample her creations, and he'd reward her with a kiss. They would share a blanket on the couch as they watched movies. And then he'd carry her off to bed and make love to her until they both collapsed from exhaustion.

The images flashed forward at a dizzying pace. He could see welcoming guests into his condo for a dinner party. He could see them snoozing in a hammock in Hawaii. Then the images started going in an unfamiliar direction that quickened his pulse. He could see her stomach full and round with their child, could see her holding a baby, surrounded by several children, the two of them as happy as his parents had been.

He snapped his eyes open with a start. His breath came

in quick pants as though he'd just sprinted around a track. When he'd thought about a future with Lia, he'd never expected it to go there. Marriage? Children?

But when he looked down at her again, a peace settled over him, calming his racing heart and slowing his breath. Yes, he could see that kind of life with her. She made it so easy for him to fall so hard for her. He just hoped the restaurant deal wouldn't destroy his chances of obtaining it.

She stirred in her sleep, and he glanced at his watch. Two o'clock. Time for him to wake her so she could make it to La Arietta in time for the dinner crowd. "Lia," he murmured, "it's time to go."

Her lashes fluttered, revealing the deep green of her drowsy gaze as she looked up at him. A sleepy smile spread across her lips. "*Ti amo*," she said in the slurred voice of the still-dreaming.

He touched her cheek. "And what does that mean?"

Her pupils constricted, erasing the last traces of sleep from her gaze, and her brows pulled together to create a single line above her nose. "Huh?"

"Never mind." He tilted her chin up so he could kiss her lips. "You were talking in your sleep."

She sat up and stretched. "I'm sorry. I didn't mean to fall asleep."

"Don't apologize. It's a good to know we can actually sleep next each other without having torn each other's clothes off beforehand."

She chuckled, a wash of deep pink flooding her cheeks. "I agree."

As he watched her, snapshots of them together in the future flashed in front of him, distracting him from the here and now. He rubbed his eyes to clear them from his sight. "I regretfully inform you that it is just past two."

The smile fell from her lips. "Which means I have to go."

He crawled toward her, grinning as he said, "Of course, you could just play hooky for the rest of the day."

"Sorry, but my name is not Ferris Bueller, and I don't get a day off." She gave him a playful shove and rose to her feet.

He followed her, taking a moment to throw everything back into the basket. "We should do this again some time."

Her shoulders tensed and her eyes widened. Her gaze moved up and down his face before she relaxed into a nod. "Yes, we should." She took the blanket from him and draped it over her arm.

The house was dry and cool after the humid heat of the afternoon, but lonely and empty. He'd grown up here and couldn't remember a moment where he and his brothers weren't running through the halls. Even after they'd all grown up and moved out, there was still Jasper galloping from room to room, trailing his mother or any houseguest who might have come over. What good was a big house if there was no one to fill it?

They were at the door before he realized it. Lia paused, her hand on the door, and leaned over to brush her lips on his cheek. "Thank you for a lovely afternoon, Adam."

The glance she gave him as she left told him she hoped

to see him again soon.

As she drove off, he pulled out his phone and found the translator app. He set it for Italian to English and repeated the words she'd said earlier. "*Ti amo.*"

"I love you," a proper feminine computerized voice replied.

The blood rushed from his head, and the bones melted from his legs. He sank down onto the stairs.

She loved him.

And he could no longer deny that he'd fallen in love with her, too.

But until he settled the restaurant problem, they didn't stand a chance.

He stared at his phone, paralyzed with fear rather than indecision. He knew what path he needed to take, and he dreaded the struggle that lay in store for him.

CHAPTER THIRTEEN

Lia wiped the sweat off her brow after adding the finishing touches to another order and watched as it was whisked into the dining room. The folded piece of paper containing her review in the *London Times* scratched against her thigh through the fabric of her pants. She reached into her pocket, holding it in her fist once again to make sure it was real.

Everything this afternoon had been part of some perfect dream that had shattered the moment Adam reminded her that it was time to come to work. Her hands had trembled the entire drive into the city. Her gut told her that he would keep his promise to let La Arietta stay here, but a creeping wisp of doubt danced along the fringes of her mind, always asking her "what if."

What if Adam did choose Schlittler over her? Would she still want to be with him?

What if he did let her keep the restaurant for now, only to ask her to give it up as their relationship progressed so she could become the society wife someone like him deserved?

The prospect of finding herself locked in a gilded cage

again terrified her more than she cared to admit. Worse, the fact she'd actually toyed with the idea of going along with it to keep him sent chills into the very essence of her soul. Adam understood her love of cooking, her passion for the restaurant. If he truly cared for her, he'd never ask her to give it up.

Julie used the break in the action to come stand next to her. "So, how did it go today?"

Lia had been so determined to throw herself into work that she'd gone nonstop from the moment she stepped into the kitchen. "It went...well."

Funny how she could capture all the confusing thoughts rolling around in her subconscious into one tiny word.

"Well? Or *well*-well?" Julie raised her brows suggestively.

"Just well. No hanky-panky involved."

Her sous chef gave a dramatic sigh. "And here I was hoping to hear all about your afternoon delight."

Lia giggled and bumped Julie's hip with her own. "It was just a picnic in his backyard, sweet and romantic."

"As opposed to the way you took off with him last night and came back with your hair all tangled up."

Lia's hand flew to her hair as though it were still a tangled mess. She smoothed it out and tried to remain calm. "I have no idea what you're talking about."

"Oh, get over it, Lia. Dax and I both know you two are into each other."

Thankfully Julie had enough sense not to broadcast to the rest of the kitchen what she really meant. Restaurants were worse than high schools when it came to the rumor mill. "Yes, we're seeing each other, and I thank you for agreeing to open today so I could have lunch with him."

"No worries." Julie started to walk off, but paused and added, "You know, I'm really glad you found someone who makes you smile."

"Smile?"

"Yeah. I mean for the last year, you've come in here every day we've been open, working so hard to make this place a success, but you never really lit up until you started seeing him, if that makes any sense."

It made too much sense. She'd mended her broken heart back together with cooking, but it had still remained empty until she'd found someone to open it up to again.

A new batch of orders came in, destroying any time she had to reflect on this discovery. The evening passed in waves of orders and entrees, dishes and desserts. Before she knew it, it was closing time. She was in the middle of assigning clean up tasks to the staff when she spotted Adam leaning against the wall outside her office.

She stepped away from the bustle of the kitchen and pulled him inside. "How did you get in here?"

"Staff entrance." He pointed to the back door that led to another stairwell and the ever-so-important trash chute. "Dax looked ready to jump me when I tried to come into the kitchen through the dining room last night."

She snickered. "Dax wants to jump you, but not in the way you're talking about."

"Too bad for him, I'm already spoken for." He pulled her into his arms and gave her a kiss that left her breathless and wanting to pull him into the stairwell for a repeat of last night.

The sound of someone clearing their throat ended the kiss before things got too out of hand. Julie stood in the doorway holding a clipboard and wearing a know-it-all grin. "You're becoming a familiar face around here, Adam."

"Would you believe I'm crazy about the cooking?"

"Who can blame you?" Her grin widened as she scribbled something on the clipboard. "I've finished assigning the closing tasks, Lia. Why don't you get out a bit early for a change?"

"I think that's fabulous idea, don't you?" Adam reached around cupped his hand firmly on her ass. "Julie looks like she has things under control."

It was a conspiracy. They must have coordinated a rendezvous point to coerce her into going home with him an hour earlier than normal. And their plan was working. She peeked at Julie's notes. "Make sure you put all the receipts in the safe."

"Got it," she replied with an efficient check mark.

"And double-check to make sure all the food is properly stored."

"Done."

"And—"

Adam cut her off by taking her hands in his own and placing them on his chest. "Lia, I think Julie knows the evening routine by now."

She'd trusted Julie to open for her today, just like she'd trusted Julie to close for her on those rare nights she ceded control of La Arietta to her sous chef. Tonight should be no different, but she still felt like she was abandoning her child in a way. The more demands Adam made of her time, the less she could dedicate to her business.

But tonight, she was willing to let go of the uptight side of her nature and enjoy her new passion—Adam. "It's your ship, captain," she told Julie as she relaxed into him.

"Woo-hoo!" Julie jumped up into the air and ran back into the kitchen. Lia listened carefully as her sous chef continued the closing routine the exact same way she normally did.

Adam guided her chin back to him. "See? Nothing to worry about."

"You're right." She unfastened her chef's jacket and switched it for the denim one she'd worn to work. "Is there any reason why you came over tonight?"

"Yes, but I'll tell you later. Right now, I just want to get you home." He leaned closer to her, his breath grazing her ear as his voice lowered. "When we get there, I'm going to remove all your clothing and explore every inch of your body from the top of your head to the tips of your toes." He paused, pulling her hips forward so the evidence of his arousal pressed against her. "With lots of intermittent stops along the way."

His arousal was so infectious, she was ready to let him begin his exploration right then and there. Her skin tingled with anticipation. "Then let's be on our way."

The drive to his place was short enough that she managed to keep her hands to herself. All restraint disappeared once they got into the elevator, though. She kissed him the same fast and frenzied way he'd done last night. Tonight, she was the one who needed him. She was the one who was tempted to press the stop button in the elevator and find her release before they even made it to his front door.

The ding announcing they'd reached his floor resurrected what was left of her self-control. She pulled away, giving him her best seductive grin.

"Patience," he said, unlocking the door to his condo. "I meant what I said about taking my time making love to you tonight."

Making love?

She'd barely had time to comprehend the meaning of the words before a hundred pounds of white fur knocked her to ground. The combination of sniffs and licks would've been enough to trigger a panic attack in most people, but Lia wedged her hands between her and the Grand Pyrenees and giggled. "There's got to be a less aggressive way to greet me, Jasper."

"Sorry, Lia," Adam grunted, tugging on the dog's collar. "I forgot that he seems to be overly fond of you."

She sat up and wiped the doggy drool off her face. "Is it just me?"

"Unfortunately." He wrestled Jasper back into the condo. "I would help you up, but I have my hands full at the moment."

"I'm fine." She stood and walked inside, scratching Jasper behind the ears as she passed. A large crate that hadn't been there a few nights ago took up a corner of the dining room. "Dog sitting?"

"Yeah, my mom's out of town, and we couldn't get a sitter at the last moment." He inched the dog closer to his crate. "Why don't you go into the bedroom while I take care of this menace for you?"

"My hero," she teased and blew him a kiss. From the other side of the door, she heard Adam playfully threatening him with Doggie Boot Camp surrounded by a bunch of yapping poodles. Jasper replied with a high-pitched bark.

The glow from his laptop screen was the only light in the room. She paused at his desk to turn on the lamp and lingered when she noticed her name on the screen.

She tried to pull herself away from the scathing e-mail someone named Raymond had sent to Adam, but her eyes continued to scan it line by line. He was threatening to sue Adam if she got the lease instead of Schlittler, calling him a fool who was thinking only with his dick. Her cheeks burned as she continued reading until the letters blurred in front of her. Then she closed her eyes and backed away until she bumped into the bed. She'd seen enough to know her relationship with Adam was creating enemies.

Her mother had always warned her that snoops never came to any good end. Once again, she wished she'd followed her mother's advice. The weight of this new knowledge pressed down on her, buckling her knees and forcing her down onto the edge of the mattress. She'd been selfish to not consider the consequences Adam faced by losing Schlittler's restaurant. But if he offered the lease to her, would she be able to accept it now that she knew what new problems she was creating for him? As much as she wanted to keep La Arietta, would it be worth knowing she'd dragged Adam into a lawsuit that could destroy his family business?

The sound of the door handle turning pulled her from her thoughts. She forced a smile on her face. The last thing Adam needed now was to know she'd been reading his private e-mail.

"I swear, if Jasper wasn't a dog, I might have to take a swing at him for jumping all over you." He shut his laptop as he passed the desk and pulled her off the bed into his arms. "Now, where were we?"

Her worries faded as his kiss coaxed her into a different world without leases and lawsuits. In this world, there was only the two of them and the promise of an evening of bliss. She surrendered to that promise as eagerly as to his touch. One by one, they removed each layer of clothing until they stood naked in each other's embrace.

Adam laid her gently on the pillows. He hovered over her, his eyes wide as though he were looking at the most beautiful woman in the world instead of her. His hands traced the curves of her body. "Where would you like me to begin?"

"Wherever you want."

"Then I'll start here." He sat back on his knees and ran his finger along her legs. When he reached her toes, he lifted her foot and brought it to his mouth.

Lia had always thought a man sucking on her toes would be kinky—or at the very least, uncomfortable—but Adam turned it into a deliciously sensual experience. Her sex tensed while she watched him give each little nub of flesh special attention, swirling his tongue around it and making her wish it was her clit he was giving such undivided attention to.

He finished with her toes and moved along her feet, placing kisses along the soles and her heels, then to the insides of her ankles. His lips continued up her calves much like he'd done that night with the raspberry sauce, only now there was less licking. Instead, his hands massaged her muscles, followed by the gentle sweep of his lips.

Upward he moved, finally reaching the place that longed for his touch. He ran his finger along her seam. Her hips rose in response, her thighs spreading open to him. Her fingers dug into the pillow. Her body wanted him to end this foreplay and move on to the highlight of the evening, but she managed to rein in her lust long enough to let him finish.

One corner of his mouth rose as he watched her. "Don't worry, Lia. I'm going to make sure you come again and again."

He lowered his head and repeated the same sucking and swirling motions on her clit as he had on her toes. The pressure inside her grew stronger and stronger with each nibble of his teeth, each lap of his tongue. Before she could stop the explosion inside her, she was arching her back and crying out his name in pleasure. But instead of stopping there with the satisfaction of knowing he'd made her come, he pressed on, drawing out her orgasm as long as he could until she was left weak and trembling beneath him.

Adam pressed his lips against the soft fullness just below her navel. "Enjoy that?"

If she opened her mouth, she was sure only incomprehensible babble would come out, so she merely nodded.

His journey continued onward, his hands caressing her hips, the small of her back, her waist, followed as always by his lips. When he came to her breasts, she'd recovered enough to let him know how much she was enjoying his attention with a series of moans and sighs. She traced her fingers along his well-muscled back, pausing to dig her nails into his skin when he took her nipples between his teeth and sent a sharp pang of pleasure straight to the lowest recesses of her pelvis.

By the time he made it to her lips, her body was demanding release. Her hips ground against him, searching for the firm rod of flesh she wanted inside her. And still, he took his time teasing her. His weight settled on her, pinning her against the mattress. His fingers threaded through hers, raising them above her head. His rigid cock pressed into her thigh, inches away from the opening of her sex. His mouth swallowed her cries of protest in a slow, easy kiss.

At last, his lips came to the top of her forehead, and he gave her a crooked grin. "Now I'm ready to make love to you properly."

He rolled off her long enough to slip a condom on. Then he slid into her with the same agonizing slowness he'd employed up to this point. Last night, they'd rushed to their climax. Tonight, he seemed determined to take his sweet time.

He built up his rhythm, sliding in and out of her with a control she wished she could master. Instead of a series of sharp jabs, his strokes were long and languid. Each one drew out the exquisite friction that made her breath catch and her stomach tighten.

"I love watching you enjoy me." He raised his hips and lowered them, reaching the deepest recesses of her sex. "I love watching your face light up as you come. I love listening to the little sounds of pleasure you make every time I slide into you."

His words proved to be as potent an aphrodisiac as his touch. Her pulse quickened, and she tightened her hold on him in preparation of the wild rush she knew awaited her when she came. "I love that fact you want to make love to me like this," she whispered.

His body shuddered against her, and his voice bore the strain of his control. "Oh, Lia, I want every night to be like this—just you and me."

"So do I."

Her response seemed to break the restraint he'd shown all evening. His movements became quicker, more erratic. He shifted his hips, changing the angle of penetration so it hit the one spot that would send her over the edge. She squeezed her arms around him, gulping for air, gritting her teeth as she foolishly tried to delay the inevitable. But it was all for naught. Her orgasm boiled up inside her and erupted with a bone-shivering vengeance.

"So beautiful, Lia." Adam's pace sped up, finally seeking his own release. "So beautiful when you come."

Then his words morphed into a low groan, and he
stilled. His jaw fell slack. A look of bliss washed over his
features. "Oh, God, Lia," he said in a hoarse whisper
before collapsing on top of her.

She held him as his body twitched with the last waves
of his release, stroking his hair and wondering when
exactly she'd fallen completely head-over-heels in love
with Adam Kelly.

****

A touch as light as angel wings pulled Adam from the
abyss of ecstasy. He inhaled Lia's scent, the sweet notes of
peaches reviving his weary muscles. As much as he
enjoyed coming inside her, it was the quiet moments in
her arms afterward that he looked forward to.

He propped himself up on his elbows and soaked in
the radiance of her face, trying to find the right words to
express the jumble of emotions swirling inside his chest.

"Satisfied?" she asked.

"For now." He rolled to the side, taking her with him
so they were lying together the exact same way they had
this afternoon. Her soft hair fanned out across his arm,
and her leg draped over his thigh. *Perfect. Things couldn't get
more perfect than this.*

Except there was more he wanted to say to her. His
gaze drifted over the closed laptop on his desk and the
angry e-mail he'd received from Ray after Adam told him
he was going to renew Lia's lease. Doubt had plagued him
all the way from his condo to La Arietta. Had he made the
right choice? Would giving Lia what she wanted be worth
the risk of lawsuits and the loss of investment capital Ray

could provide?

But once he saw her in action, his mind eased. Lia was in her element in the kitchen. Her cheeks glowed with excitement as she prepared one dish after another, her eyes following each plate as it went out the door like a proud parent. He'd stood there in the back of the kitchen for almost half an hour before she finally noticed him, but the glimpse he'd gotten settled any lingering questions he had. He couldn't give her the moon, but he could give her the one thing she loved above everything else.

Adam had planned on telling her tonight, but he feared ruining the moment if he brought up the subject right now. Instead, he focused on matching the rise and fall of his chest to hers. "I could die a happy man right now."

She threw her arm around his chest and hugged him. "Me, too."

His heart squeezed tighter. Lia had become the one thing he desired more than anything in his whole life. "I want to spend every night like this, Lia, with you lying next to me."

She lifted her head from his chest, her lips parted and her brows drawn together. She searched his face as her fingers trailed along his chest, finally settling over his heart. A small smile appeared. "And you always get what you want."

"Yes, as long as you're willing to stay here."

The crease reappeared above her nose. What had he said that caused her concern?

Before he could ask, his phone rang. This time, however, it was Bates's ringtone. What would possess him to call this late at night?

A second ring tone pierced the silence, and Lia jumped. The two phones continued to ring, each one echoing the other, demanding their attention until Adam grabbed his and stepped into the living room. "What is it, Bates?"

Lia's phone stopped ringing as well, followed by the hushed sound of her voice as she answered.

"Mr. Kelly, there's been a fire in the Michigan Avenue property."

CHAPTER FOURTEEN

A sheen of sweat broke out over his skin. "Where in the building?"

"The top floor, from what I've been told." *Shit! La Arietta.* He sucked in a breath and held it, praying he'd heard Bates wrong. "I'm en route now to see if I can get in and assess the damage."

"I'll meet you there." He hung up and stood outside his bedroom door, listening for Lia. When no sound came from the room, he gently pressed on the door to open it.

Lia sat on the edge of the bed, the phone cradled in her hands. Wet lines streaked down her pale face. She stared straight ahead like a statue, letting her tears fall.

A crushing sensation of helplessness engulfed him. If he could wave a magic wand, the spell he'd cast would keep her from ever learning the truth about the fire. Instead, he settled for the role of being the person she could lean on in this time of trouble. He found her clothes and laid them next to her. "Lia, let's get dressed and go see the damage."

Her shoulders shook, lightly at first but quickly growing into a sob that wracked her entire body. He sat next to her and held until her initial grief passed and the flow of her scalding tears ebbed.

"We'll get through this together, Lia," he whispered. "I promise."

She lifted her head with a sniff and wiped her face with the back of her hand. "You're right, Adam. Crying doesn't help anything." She slipped her panties up over her hips. "Let's go and see what's left."

The calm of her voice belied the droop of her shoulders, the half-hearted effort in which she dressed. She rode down the elevator with her arms wrapped around her waist, hugging herself while she stood several feet away from him. Her face remained void of emotion as they drove to the restaurant and the sea of flashing red lights that greeted them when they arrived.

After explaining to the firemen that they were the owners, they were allowed to enter the parking garage and go up to the top floor.

The acrid stench of smoke filled his nostrils as they got closer to La Arietta. A gasp broke free from her lips when the elevator doors parted. The fire may not have consumed the entire restaurant, but the damage was enough to call it a total loss. Smoke stains blackened the ceiling of the lobby, and wet plaster dripped off the walls. Beyond them, the charred remains of tables and chairs stood like ghastly skeletons at the far end of the dining room near the kitchen door.

Bates approached them, his eyes flickering to Lia before speaking. "It's not as bad as I first thought."

If Lia heard his words, she gave no indication.

Bates gave him a quick jerk of his head, indicating there was more he wanted to say in private.

Adam squeezed her hand. "Will you be okay here for moment?"

She nodded, her gaze still fixed straight ahead.

"I didn't want to upset Ms. Mantovani any more than she already is." Bates led him into the heart of the once-vibrant dining room, stopping at the line of black on the tile floor that marked the edge of the flames near the kitchen door. "From what I gather, the fire started in the kitchen near the deep fryer. The inspector is already investigating the cause as we speak."

As if on cue, a man emerged from the kitchen deep in conversation with one of the firemen. He scribbled a few notes on his clipboard and nodded before coming toward them. "Are you Mr. Kelly?"

Adam nodded. "Is the building safe?"

"You wouldn't have been able to come in if it wasn't." The inspector made a few more notes. "I'll have to look at the levels below before I can make the final call on whether they'll be safe for people to return to work or not."

"I'll call the smoke and water damage crew and have them here in the morning," Bates offered.

Adam waited for the inspector to answer the one question plaguing his mind, but when he didn't offer the information, he asked, "Any clue as to the cause?"

"Looks like a faulty plug above the fryer." He held up a charred, twisted mess of metal and plastic. "A few sparks from that thing, and the oil would have ignited like gunpowder. Classic grease fire."

"I'm glad the firemen were able to contain it so quickly."

"Yeah, me too. Makes my job simpler." He dropped the evidence into a plastic bag and sealed it. "Now, let's take a look below."

"Bates, you take him. I'll stay here with Lia."

The two men disappeared into the stairwell, and Adam faced the ominous task of trying to console the woman he loved.

****

Lia took a few steps and halted, her chin quivering as she took it all in. It was all ruined. Everything she'd poured her heart and soul into for the last year was now sopping wet and reeking of smoke. Every dime she'd invested into La Arietta had gone up in flames, leaving her nothing.

A flash of light called to her, and she crossed the lobby to where the framed issue of *Food and Wine* hung on the wall, still dry behind the pane of glass. She took it down and hugged it. Even if she never rebuilt La Arietta, she had proof that it had been real, that she'd created something wonderful and marvelous and....

Her thoughts choked up in a silent sob. It didn't matter what it had been. Now it was all gone.

A pair of warm hands rested on her shoulders. "It'll be all right, Lia," Adam said in a gentle voice meant to soothe her. "We can rebuild it."

"No, we can't." A new batch of tears threatened to spill over. "I don't have the money. My fire policy will barely cover the repairs needed to get it back to usable condition. It won't replace the furniture or the appliances or the lost income."

He pulled her into his arms and made a few shushing noises. "Don't worry about the money."

A spark of fury ignited deep inside her chest, spreading as quickly as the fire in the restaurant had. "That's easy for someone like you to say. You've never had to worry about how to make ends meet or how you're going to afford to move out of your mother's apartment while still keeping your business afloat."

"Then what do you want me to say?" he asked, his arms falling to his sides.

"I don't know," she admitted, hugging the framed magazine even tighter. "If you offer to lend me the money to reopen La Arietta, then I'd always feel indebted to you. It would feel like you owned part of my soul."

"Then are you saying you'd rather walk away from this?" He hooked his finger under her chin, increasing the pressure until she finally looked up at him. "Listen to me—I'll take care of everything—the repairs, the inspections, the paperwork. You can move in with me and never have to worry about a thing ever again."

Her gut wrenched. He was offering to take control of everything and set up her up in his home. Her pulse pounded in her temples, and her mouth went dry. It was the gilded cage all over again. He wanted to lock her away and keep her from the one thing that could tear them apart.

Mr. Bates thankfully spared her from having to tell him

161

no. "Mr. Kelly, perhaps you should come downstairs and take a look before we form a plan of action."

Her throat tightened as though someone had slipped a noose around her neck. She'd overheard the inspector. A grease fire had caused all this damage. It was all her fault for not staying here and making sure everything was in order before leaving. If she'd been here, maybe she could have put the fire out before it spread. Now she'd destroyed not only her restaurant, but the surrounding businesses in Adam's building.

Adam ran his thumb over her lips. "Think about my offer."

She didn't need to think about it. She already knew her answer, but she was too much of a coward to tell him right then. She stood there while he followed Mr. Bates downstairs, forming the best plan. She couldn't resurrect La Arietta on her own, and she couldn't become a kept woman. Each beat of her heart confirmed the inevitable, deepening the ache in her chest.

She had no future with a man like Adam Kelly.

Now was the time to slip out of his life for good, before her body seized control of her better judgment and she surrendered to his touch. She pressed the button for the elevator and caught a cab home to her mother's apartment, carrying only the memories of a few shattered dreams with her.

CHAPTER FIFTEEN

Adam punched in Lia's number one more time. Like every time he'd tried to call her over the last two days, it went straight to voice mail. He hadn't heard a word from her since the fire except for a text telling him she'd gone to her mother's, followed by the e-mail he'd received less than an hour ago letting him know that he could give the lease to Amadeus Schlittler.

"Damn it, woman! Why are you being so stubborn?"

Her silence didn't just hurt—it tore at his heart like some sadistic punishment that inflicted pain every time he thought of her. He'd offered to have her move in with him and let him take of everything that worried her. In truth, it was the closest he'd come to proposing to her. Maybe he would've been better off doing that.

He pulled up the e-mail again and let her cold words prick his skin like dozens of little daggers.

> *Dear Adam,*
>
> *Seeing as how the damage to La Arietta will require extensive time and money to repair, I think it is in your best interest to offer the space to Amadeus Schlittler and forget about me.*

Sincerely,

Lia Mantovani

He slammed his keyboard against his desk in frustration. Maybe he'd been wrong in his assumption that she'd really cared for him. Maybe it had all been an act to seduce him into letting her keep the restaurant, and now that she couldn't afford it, she was done with him.

But when he remembered the way she'd told him she loved him in that sleepy voice a few days ago, he knew she hadn't been pretending. She loved him as much as he loved her. He just needed to find out what had her running scared.

A brisk knock sounded at his door. Bates came in carrying two folders. "Mr. Kelly, Mr. Volowski has been rather, um, insistent to learn your final decision on the Michigan Avenue property. I've taken the liberty of drawing up two different leases—one for Mr. Schlittler and one for Ms. Mantovani."

Bates placed each folder on his desk and opened them up to the documents inside. It was time to make a decision. He skimmed over the prospective agreement with Schlittler, then the one with Lia. He halted when he saw the monthly rent on her lease. "Is this correct?" he asked, pointing to the number that was a quarter of what he'd normally charge.

Bates put on his reading glasses and checked the figure. "Yes, sir. That is the amount in her original sublease."

"Who authorized it?"

His assistant flipped past the new lease to reveal the original one. On the very last page, the delicate loops of his mother's signature filled the owner's line.

Adam took a deep breath and leaned back in his chair. He should've known there was one more piece of the puzzle that he'd overlooked. "I think I need to have a conversation with the *owner* before I do anything else."

"And what should I tell Mr. Volowski when he calls again?"

Adam stared at Schlittler's lease, then Lia's. He'd promised her he'd do everything in his power to let her keep La Arietta. If he wanted to win her back, he needed to start by proving he was a man of his word.

He picked up Schlittler's lease and tore it in half. "Tell Mr. Volowski that Chef Amadeus and I failed to reach an agreement."

Bates raised a brow but took the shredded paper without asking why. A faint smile played on his lips. "Very good, sir. I'll arrange a lunch date with your mother when she returns to Chicago on Tuesday."

"Thank you." He closed the folder with Lia's leases and patted the cover. It was a start, but he could take it one step further. "Also, could you please find the photos you took of La Arietta before the fire and show them to the contractor? I want everything restored to the way it was."

"Right away, Mr. Kelly." Bates nodded in approval, adding before he shut door behind him, "By the way, Robert Curry called and has asked to set up a meeting with you. Said he found what you were looking for."

Adam cracked his knuckles. Time to deliver the one-two blow, especially if Curry's cryptic message meant he had the dirt on Ray. He picked up the phone and dialed

Curry's number. "I understand you'd like to set up a meeting?"

The private investigator chuckled. "I went digging like you asked, and you won't believe the sewer line I hit."

He grinned. "That bad, huh?"

"Worse."

He checked the clock on his desk. Three o'clock. Normally, he'd be counting down the minutes until he saw Lia again by this time of day, but now he itched to learn what Curry had unearthed and how he could use it against Ray. "When can you be here?"

"I'm just a couple of blocks down the road from your office."

"What a coincidence—I happen to have an opening in my schedule right now. I'll tell Bates to let you in when you arrive."

"See you in a few." The phone clicked dead, but it didn't kill Adam's enthusiasm.

He buzzed Bates. "Hold off on letting Ray know my decision. I'll deliver it to him personally after I meet with Mr. Curry."

"Very good, sir."

At least there was one thing going in his favor. Adam glanced at the e-mail on his screen again. If she wouldn't answer his phone calls, then hopefully she'd read her e-mail. He clicked the reply arrow and started typing. Business first, and once that was settled, then hopefully he could go back to the pleasure of having her in his arms once again.

****

The phone buzzed in her lap again. She looked at the number and silenced it.

"It's him again, isn't it?" her mother asked as she took the off ramp for O'Hare Airport.

"What does it matter?" She'd made her break with him, much like yanking a bandage off in one swift stroke. Yes, it stung, but the pain would be over sooner than slowly drawing it out.

"Maybe he has something to say to you."

She stared out the window at the tails of all the planes lining the terminals. "He's said enough for me to realize he's no different than Trey."

"Bullshit. No son of Maureen Kelly would ever be like that arrogant prick. She raised them better than that, just like I raised you better than the way you're acting now."

Lia closed her eyes and counted to ten before her temper got the better of her and resulted in her mother making a U-turn back to their apartment. "I told you before—I just need some space to figure out what I'm going to do next."

"No, you're running away from your problems, and I'm ashamed of you."

"Ma, please, just let me deal with it."

"But you're not dealing with it. You should be back there at your restaurant starting the repair work, not catching a plane to mope around Italy with my cousin."

Lia pressed her fingers to her temples. "It's not that simple. For starters, I don't own that space any more. My lease ends today."

"So you assume." She pointed at Lia's phone, swerving

into the next lane as she did and earning a blaring reprimand from someone's horn. "Maybe that's what Adam's been trying to tell you all morning, but you're too pessimistic to answer him and hear what he has to say."

"No, that's not what it's about." She drew in a deep breath, knowing her confession would probably earn her a swat across the back of her head...and probably have her mom veering off the road in a fit of rage. "I gave up the space."

"What?" The rear tires of her mother's 1992 sedan squealed, and the steering wheel resembled one of those carnival rides that spun back and forth without any rhyme or reason.

Lia straight-armed the dashboard and prayed she'd make it to the terminal alive.

The car rocked from side to side as her mother found the center of the lane again. Her lips formed a thin line, and the furrows in her brow spoke more harshly of her displeasure than any lecture ever could. "There's something you're not telling me, isn't there?"

"Yes, Ma, there is."

"You're not knocked up, are you?"

Lia's jaw dropped. "What kind of accusation is that?"

"Why else would you give up the thing you loved the most unless you knew you had a little one on the way?" The anger in her face melted into the exciting prospect of possibly becoming a grandmother. "Why didn't I think of that sooner?"

"Keep dreaming, Ma. There is no baby." As evidenced by the monthly reminder that she'd wasted another egg this morning. Someone said confession was good for the soul, so since she was baring it all to her mother, she continued, "Someone was threatening to sue Adam if he renewed my lease."

"And you think he isn't man enough to stand up for you, huh?"

"No, I—" What would Adam have done if La Arietta hadn't caught on fire? Would he have renewed her lease and faced the consequences without telling her? Would he have bowed down to pressure? She glanced down at the phone, wondering if she should even bother asking him. "Jules is already looking at places for me, and when I get back, I'll make a decision on what the next step will be for La Arietta."

The car pulled up to the curb in front of her airline. Her gaze flew from the phone to the ticket counter and back again. She closed her eyes and prayed for an answer. Instead, all she heard was Adam telling her she could move in with him and never have to worry about a thing. If she believed in signs, that would be the one alerting her that he didn't really know who she was. She turned her phone off and tucked it into her purse.

"Bye, Ma." She reached over to give her mom a quick hug and a kiss goodbye. "I'll call you when I get to Carolina's."

Her mother sat in the driver's seat, her arms crossed. "It's your life, Lia."

Which meant she thought Lia was making a huge mistake.

Lia got out of the car and tugged her suitcase from the

backseat. "Yes, it is my life, and I'm making the best decision I can at the moment." Her chest ached when she acknowledged that it meant giving up Adam in the process. "It's what's best for both of us," she whispered before slamming the door shut.

CHAPTER SIXTEEN

"Good afternoon, dear." His mother leaned over, surrounding him in a cloud of Chanel No. 5, and kissed his forehead. "So good to see you again. How's Jasper been?"

"Moping all week." *Much like me.* He waited until his mother sat down across the table from him at the tiny little French café she adored. "I'll bring him by the house tonight."

"Thank you so much for dog-sitting at the last minute. You know how I loathe putting him in a kennel."

"You spoil that dog way more than you ever did any of us."

"That's because all my boys have grown up, left the house and haven't given me any grandbabies to fill the void."

Adam inwardly groaned. Not the guilt trip again. Instead, he pulled out the folder containing Lia's lease. "I stumbled across something very interesting while you were away."

His mother pulled out her Kate Spade reading glasses and skimmed the contract. "Oh, that. I was wondering when you'd make your mind up. Have you told Lia the news?"

"I will, if I can ever get hold of her." He pulled out the prior contract and flipped to the last page bearing his mother's signature. "I wanted to know about the original deal you struck with her."

She removed her glasses and took a sip of the wine he'd ordered for her. "You know Emilia and I are dear friends. When she mentioned to me last year that her daughter wanted to open a restaurant but was having trouble finding a location, I thought I'd be nice and offer her that space."

Little warning bells went off in the back of his mind. His mother rarely meddled in the family business unless she had ulterior motives. "At a quarter of its normal rent?"

"Now you're just exaggerating." She squinted at the amount on the original contract. "Yes, I agree it's at a discount, but it was a sublet. I figured it was something she could afford just starting out, and it wasn't doing us any good after that night club broke their original lease with us."

"Why didn't you run any of this by me?" He crossed his arms and zeroed his gaze in on her.

She smiled sweetly, not at all intimidated by his stance. "Adam, dear, you may have taken over running the business when your father passed away, but I'm still legally the owner." She raised her glass to her lips, her grin widening.

His jaw tightened. He had no rebuttal for that argument. "So if I had terminated her lease for Schlittler?"

"I would have stepped in and vetoed your decision. After all, I am the owner, and you're basically my property manager."

His mother had spent so many years raising a family and playing the role of society wife that he'd forgotten she was a truly intelligent woman behind the polished veneer, a woman who'd gone to law school and was interning at one of the top law firms in Chicago when she'd met his father.

Maybe that's why he could never win an argument with her.

The waiter interrupted their conversation to take their orders. His mother gave hers without even looking at the menu while he mumbled that he'd take the special—some sort of crepes with ham and cheese. He really didn't care what he ate. None of it compared to Lia's food.

Once the waiter left, his mother tapped on the folder. "I take it you're going to renew her lease then. What changed your mind?"

Her question seemed innocent, but the tone of her voice in combination with the knowing light in her eyes hit him like a sucker punch. The last month had all been one big setup orchestrated by his mother. He sucked in a breath, held it until his temper simmered down, and slowly exhaled before he dared to ask, "Let me guess—you didn't win a charity auction."

"I don't know what you're talking about." His mother checked her reflection in her spoon, patting her hair as though one of the meticulously styled strands had moved out of place.

"That dinner at the lake house—you arranged it."

She said nothing, but the corner of her mouth rose ever so slightly.

His fingers curled into his palm. "And I suppose Lia was in on it, too?"

"No, no, no." A look of panic flashed across his mother's face. "Lia was as innocent as you were, dear. Emilia and I thought we could create a situation where her daughter could be introduced to several of my sons and see if there were any sparks."

Sparks was putting it mildly. Try full-blown inferno. "And where does her lease fit into this?"

"Well, I was hoping once you met her and tasted her cooking, you'd think twice about shutting her down." She set her spoon back down, nudging it until it was perfectly aligned with the rest of the silverware on the table. "But when I saw the chemistry between you two when you first met, well, I...."

"It's kind of hard to have chemistry with someone while dragging a big hairy dog off of her."

His mother hid her laugh behind her hand. "I knew that if Jasper loved her, one of my boys would, too."

A pain formed in his chest, growing more intense with every beat of his heart until he was forced to close his eyes. And when he did, he saw Lia's face after he'd made love to her that last night. Yes, his mother had been right. One of her boys had fallen in love with her.

She was watching him with her head tilted slightly to the side, one brow arched as though she were waiting for his confession as he opened his eyes.

"I hate to disappoint you, Mom, but don't get your hopes up too high. Lia's refusing to answer my calls now."

Her lips parted, and her eyes widened. "What did you do?"

"Why do you think I did something?" The ache in his chest turned to fire. "She's the one who disappeared the night of the fire and hasn't spoken to me since, other than to send me an e-mail telling me to give the space to Schlittler. I have no idea where she is, what's she doing, how she's dealing with the loss, or what I might have done to make her act this way. I've gotten nothing but silence."

"Well, that simply won't do." She pulled out her cell phone and dialed a number. "Hello, Emilia, how are you?" A pause, followed by nodding. "Funny you should mention that. I'm having lunch with Adam right now. He's missing Lia something fierce."

It rankled him that he had to go to his mother for the information he needed, but if it meant he could find Lia and get some answers, he'd suffer the brief moment of humiliation that poked at the edges of his mind.

The conversation continued for another minute with more sounds of agreement before his mother pulled a pen out of her purse. "Now, what is that address?" She scribbled something on the folder and handed it back to Adam, a triumphant smile on her face.

The words all appeared to be part of a foreign language except for the last one. Italy.

"Oh, did he now?" His mother gave him her accusatory glare, one he hadn't seen since she'd gotten a call from his high school principal after he'd organized and carried out the senior prank. "No, I won't say a thing about that. He's a big enough boy to figure it out on his own."

Shit. His mother knew something that would make his life infinitely easier, and she was holding out on him. Maybe he'd be able to weasel it out of her once she got off the phone.

Of course, she already knew what he was thinking and changed the conversation. "You know, I stumbled across a new strategy that we could use next time we play Judy and Karl."

Oh, sure, talk about bridge when I'm sitting on the edge of my seat to find out what you know. Thanks, Mom.

She continued to talk about jump-reverses and trump leads until the waiter set a salad down in front of her. "We'll have to get together later this week and try it out. Well, lunch is here. I've got to go for now." She paused, listening to something Lia's mother said, shaking her head. "No, don't tell her. She's equally as stubborn as Adam, and we've done more than enough."

She turned her phone off and slipped it back into her purse. "This looks delicious."

Hardly. The salad in front of him remained untouched. "What did you learn, Mom?"

"Exactly what I showed you." She pointed her fork to the address on the folder. "If you want to find Lia, she's there."

"And did her mom give you any clue why Lia won't return my calls and went to Italy?"

His mother stopped chewing. A brief glimpse at her

inner struggle flickered across her features, from the twitch of her eyes to the harder-than-normal swallow. "I don't want to interfere in your personal life."

"It's too late for that. You're the one who thought it would be a great idea to play matchmaker." He leaned forward, his elbows propped on the table in a way that would've earned him a scolding when he was growing up. "I want to make things right with her, and it would help to know what I'm up against before getting on the next plane to Italy."

"So you are going to go after her?"

He glanced down at the folder and then back at his mom. The easy thing to do would be to let her go, to acknowledge that they both loved their jobs too much to ever truly be comfortable with each other as long as her restaurant sat in his building. But that wasn't what he wanted, not now. And if it meant he had to go to her on his knees and beg for forgiveness for whatever he'd unconsciously done to offend her, he'd do it. "Yes."

His mother beamed with contained joy for a few seconds before growing serious. "Did Lia ever tell you why she went to Italy in the first place four years ago?"

"She said her fiancé cheated on her, and she wanted to make a fresh start." He racked his brain trying to figure out what that had to do with them. "I didn't do that."

"I know you didn't, but you have to remember that Lia is very proud, and very determined not to find herself in the same position where she's dependent on someone else. She's put so much of herself into her restaurant that she'd be at a loss if she were forced to give it up."

"And I don't want her to give it up. I've even authorized repairs to the space so it'll be exactly as she had it before the fire."

"Then perhaps you should tell her that." She shoved the folder toward him. "Shall I have Bates schedule your flight while you pack?"

He tucked the folder containing the leases into his briefcase, making a mental note to stop by the building and take pictures of the repair process so far. "That sounds like a good plan."

"Excellent. Now, I need your help dealing with Ben." His mother launched into a new conversation about how worried she was about his brother, but he only half listened. His thoughts were occupied by the green-eyed chef on the other side of the world.

By this time tomorrow, he'd be in Italy.

And with any luck, he'd have Lia back in his arms.

CHAPTER SEVENTEEN

"That's enough, Carolina." Lia yanked the jar filled with red pepper flakes away from her mother's cousin. "You don't want your guests biting into a fireball."

"But I like it spicy." Carolina grabbed a pinch more from the open jar and sprinkled it over the mixture of ground chicken and ricotta cheese that comprised the filling for the ravioli they were making. "Remember, it's my kitchen."

As if she could forget. Carolina ruled over the massive kitchen like a queen over a small province. Here she was the master, and Lia was the student. But that didn't mean the pupil couldn't make a few small tweaks here and there.

Carolina peered over Lia's shoulder at the pale green sheet of pasta rolling out of the press. "What did you put in the dough?"

"A little pureed basil."

The queen threw her hands up in the air and muttered a string of curses in Italian, followed by an overly dramatic monologue about how children had no respect for their elders and tradition.

But that couldn't be farther from the truth. Lia had

nothing but respect for the traditional dishes her mother's cousin prepared. It was here she'd first learned the art of Italian cooking. It was here where she'd discovered her passion. And it was here she'd found solace after life dealt her another series of blows to her love life.

Only this time, she didn't find the escape she sought. Adam constantly lingered in her mind. She missed his smile. She missed his self-deprecating humor. She missed the touch of his lips on her skin. She missed falling asleep in his arms. And with each passing day, she began to wonder if she'd made a mistake in seeing the world in black and white terms. There was a chance she could have had both her passions—Adam and La Arietta—but her pride kept her from seeing it that way before she left. Now, in the laid-back world of Italy, she began to see possibilities she'd never considered, scenarios where she could have it all. And maybe, once she got La Arietta up and running again in a new location, she could try to pick up the pieces with Adam.

That is, if it wasn't too late.

Nick, Carolina's younger son, rambled down the stairs. "What did you do this time, Lia?" he asked with a wink before placing a soothing kiss on his mother's forehead

"Just made a slight improvement to tonight's menu." She held out the thin sheet of dough for him. "I didn't trigger the fall of the Roman Empire or anything like that."

"She is always changing something." Carolina pointed a gnarled finger at Lia. "You'd think she was here to take over my kitchen."

The thought was tempting. She could turn the family's *agriturismo* into a world-class dining experience and not give La Arietta a second thought. But she also knew she'd never wrestle control of the kitchen from Carolina as long as her mother's cousin lived.

And Italy was too far away from the man she loved.

"Lia's an accomplished chef, Mama. She's only trying to please our guests with something that will surely be delicious." He came by Lia and whispered so his mother couldn't overhear, "Not to mention it has been a step above what we've been serving. You have to write some of this down for me so I can continue doing it once you leave."

She didn't envy Nick. Shortly after she'd arrived four years ago, Lia had convinced her family to buy an old sixteenth-century estate and turn it into an *agriturismo*, a working farm that doubled as a bed and breakfast for visitors. Nick's brother, Giovanni, revived the ancient Sangiovese vines and started producing a wine that was already getting rave reviews from tasters. Nick took over the accommodation part of the business, seeing to the guests' needs and making sure the rooms were booked well in advance.

It also involved appeasing the diva chef on site.

"I'll start a diary for you," she said and stretched the fresh dough out on the sturdy wooden table. "We're ready for the filling, Carolina."

Her mother's cousin cradled the bowl like a child, unwilling to part with it. "You promise not to make any more changes to tonight's dinner?"

Lia crossed her fingers behind her back so only Nick could see them. "Of course."

She just wouldn't let Carolina know about the fresh summer savory and tarragon that she'd added to the rub for the chicken they were planning on roasting.

Nick drew them together, his arms around their shoulders. "I'm the luckiest man in the world to have two such talented cooks working for me."

His compliment soothed his mother's ruffled feathers, and Carolina began dropping spoonfuls of the filling on the dough. When she came to the end of the sheet, Lia covered them with another sheet of dough and pressed the two layers together, carefully removing any air from them that could cause the ravioli to explode during cooking.

Carolina glanced down her nose and nodded in approval when Lia had finished. "Yes, that will do. The basil might even balance out the pepper."

Lia grinned and ran a pizza cutter along the sheet, cutting it up into individual squares. One battle at a time.

She was just finishing up the third batch of ravioli when she heard a familiar voice asking in stilted Italian, "*Dov'è Lia?*"

Her heart stutter-stepped to a halt. She turned to the stairs that led to the lobby of the manor house just in time to see a pair of polished black leather shoes descend into view. A second later she saw Adam, immaculately dressed in a tailored suit that made his shoulders seem broader than ever.

Their eyes met. He stopped a few steps from the

kitchen, staring at her as though he hadn't seen her in years.

Her pulse pounded in her ears, and her hands suddenly felt clumsy. She wiped them on her apron, fully aware of the audience of relatives who'd filtered in around them. "Adam, what are you doing here?"

"I—" His voice cracked, and he turned away to grab something from his briefcase. "I wanted to talk to you about this."

He held out a folder, and something collapsed inside her chest. He was here for business, not her. She looked down at her flour-covered hands. "Give me a moment to clean up, and I'll meet you outside."

He nodded and retreated up the stairs. Unfortunately, the family didn't follow. Carolina's two daughters crowded around her at the sink. "Who's he?" Sophia asked in Italian.

"Yes, he's hot," Estella added. "If you don't want him, can I give him my number?"

"The American is here to see Lia, not you silly girls." Carolina shooed them away and held out a clean towel. "Remember that pride often closes our eyes, our ears, and our hearts. Don't forget to ask and to listen."

Lia took the towel and dried her hands, wondering how much her mother had shared with her cousin while Lia was on the plane. Her breath calmed, and a new feeling of peace surrounded her. Surely, Adam wouldn't have come all the way here just to deliver the termination of her contract. *"Grazie mille, Zia Carolina."*

She took the steps one at a time, bolstering her courage

183

as she rose into the lobby. Nick was trying to engage Adam in a lighthearted conversation while Sophia and Estella pretended to be cleaning, their dark gazes fixed on Adam as they worked. When they saw her, they stopped and giggled, retreating into the next room. Carolina hobbled up the stairs and leaned against the wall. They were all watching her to see what happened next.

Adam glanced at the audience gathered around them. "Is there some place where we can talk privately?"

"This way." She led him out the back door toward the farmyard, casting one glare over her shoulder at her family as she closed the door behind him. If they dared follow, she'd give them a tongue-lashing that would make even Carolina blush.

Three chickens dashed past Adam, stopping him in his tracks. He raised his briefcase up to his shoulders, far out the squawking poultry's reach. "What kind of place is this?"

"An *agriturismo.* The livestock are part of the whole working-farm thing." She led him to the barn and sniffed the air before inviting him in. The hay was fresh, and the cows had been in the field all day. Nothing that could offend Adam's rich city-boy senses. "Now what did you want to talk to me about?"

"Why did you leave without telling me?"

He wasted no time getting to the point, but she wasn't quite ready to give him the answers he wanted. She thought she could forget about him, but every night since the fire, she tossed and turned, wishing he'd been there to hold her in his arms. The ache was just beginning to dull.

But now that she'd seen him again, it returned full force, along with the longing, the desire, and the emotion she feared to name. To do so would only add to the weight of her heartbreak.

She strolled to one of the massive columns supporting the barn and leaned against it, her back to him. "I didn't know you owned me."

"Damn it, Lia." He was behind her faster than she realized. "What kind of game are you playing? There I was, trying to comfort you after your loss, and then you up and disappeared without a word."

She spun around, her gut churning like Lake Michigan on a windy day. "You're the one who told me give up my restaurant and move in with you."

His brows drew together. "No, I didn't."

"Yes, you did. I distinctly remember you telling me to move in with you and let you take care of me. Well, here's a newsflash, Adam. I don't need anyone to take care of me."

"That's not what I meant at all." A spark of anger flared in his deep blue eyes, and his shoulders formed a stubborn line. "I was merely trying to relieve you of the burden of dealing with the fire damage."

"By forcing me to give up the restaurant."

"Ugh, I can't believe you'd think that." He turned away from her and paced the length of the barn several times before remembering the folder in his hand. "Just take a look at this."

She opened the folder and skimmed the first page. Her chest tightened, and a warm glow ignited in the pit of her stomach. "You're renewing my lease?"

"Yes."

"B-but what about Schlittler and that man threatening to sue you?"

His eyes narrowed. "How did you know about that?"

She let the contract dangle from her fingers. As much as she still wanted it, she didn't want to have Adam deal with the repercussions. "I'm sorry, Adam, I can't sign this."

He took the papers and heaved a deep breath. "Let's start from the beginning, Lia. It seems we've both fallen victim to yet another misunderstanding, and I'm not leaving until we lay everything out on the table. Let's start with this. I want to renew your lease."

"I don't want to cause any trouble for you." She lowered her eyes, staring at the terra-cotta-colored dust on the ground. If he wanted honesty, then she at least owed him that. "I accidentally saw that e-mail about the lawsuit thing."

"And you were willing to give up your restaurant for me?" A brief glimpse of shock flashed across his face before he composed himself. "Don't worry about Ray. He's full of hot air. I've already taken care of that matter."

"How?"

"Let's just say he has several high-end call girls on his speed dial and doesn't want that information, or anything else my private investigator found on him that will jeopardize his reelection campaign, leaking out to the press." He waved the contract in front of her again. "Now that you know that, will you sign your lease?"

"I—" She licked her lips, her mouth dry with indecision. "Why would you want me over Schlittler?"

"Besides the fact you're an amazing chef and he's an ass?" He closed the space between them. The contract disappeared into his briefcase, which fell to the ground when his hands found her hips. "Let's just say I have a little thing for you."

The erection hardening inside his pants was anything but little. She circled her arms around his neck and leaned into him. Her lips found his with instinctual ease. Desire flooded her veins as the kiss deepened, making her forget about all the reasons why they'd never work out as a couple. All she cared about was here and now.

When the kiss ended, Adam asked in a raw voice, "Why did you leave me, Lia?"

"I was scared." Those three little words slipped out before she could form a more appropriate reply, but they summed up the confusing turmoil of feelings she had whenever she came near him.

"Why?" He ran his hands up and down her spine in slow, steady strokes while he waited for her answer, his gaze never wavering.

She drew in a shaky breath. "When I heard you say you wanted me to move in with you and let you take care of everything, all I could think about was the last time I found myself in that situation. I know I don't fit the mold of the perfect little housewife you deserve—"

"Who said anything about you becoming a housewife?" He placed a quick peck on the tip of her nose. "When I invited you to move in with me, I did so because I want you in my bed every night. And when I offered to make sure you'll never worry about a thing, I meant that I would handle the insurance adjusters and paperwork and permits and everything else that needed to be done to get La Arietta open once again."

He released her long enough to pull out his iPad and tap on a folder. Images of the half-repaired restaurant filled the screen. One by one, he scrolled through them for her. The plaster that had been ruined by the water had been torn down and replaced. The scorched tables and chairs had been cleared out to make room for plush seats with real leather upholstery. In the kitchen, top-of-the-line appliances gleamed under the lights. La Arietta was like a phoenix rising from the ashes, more beautiful than it had been before.

The last image was the sign that greeted people when they got off the elevator. Underneath it was a smaller sign that said "Under repair, but reopening soon."

Her throat choked up, and her eyes burned. Now it was her turn to ask why.

"Because I want you to enjoy your passion." He kissed her again, his tongue seeking confirmation of her feelings with every pleading swirl, every timid flick. "I love you, Lia."

The tears she'd been fighting to hold back spilled over. "I love you, too, Adam."

A grin flashed on his face before he pulled her back into his arms and covered her mouth with his again. All restraint vanished. It was the hallway all over again. Desperate kisses. Tugs on clothing. Roaming hands that yearned to feel flesh. Desire that overwhelmed common sense.

The straps of her sundress fell off her shoulders. Adam was tasting the newly exposed skin when the barn door opened with a bang. They flew apart like they had the night on the boat, half-naked and flushed.

Giovanni stood in the doorway, his mouth hanging open. Then a sly smile curled his lips. "What is that American saying? A roll in the hay?"

Lia pressed her burning cheeks into Adam's back. Her mother would definitely hear about this before the night was over.

Adam reached around for her hand, placing a chaste kiss on it as he pulled her strap back up. "Perhaps we should hold off until we get someplace where we won't be interrupted."

"Good idea. You know how large families can be."

"Without a doubt." A twinkle appeared in his eyes, one that spoke of many sensuous nights tangled in the sheets. "I hope you're up for the challenge."

She grinned back, running her fingers through his hair to smooth it back into place. "Absolutely. You've become my new passion."

His breath caught. A look of surprise flickered across his face, followed by an intense emotion that made her heart swell. "Then I will do all I can to keep that passion alive."

Hand in hand, they strolled back to the manor house, oblivious to the people around them. Tomorrow, they would talk business. Tomorrow, they would go over the

repairs to La Arietta and the terms of the lease.
Tomorrow, they would make plans to move her things
into his condo.

But tonight, they would enjoy the simple pleasures of
each other under the warm summer moon.

A Note to Readers

Dear Reader,

Thank you so much for reading *The Sweetest Seduction*. I hope you enjoyed it and look forward to Ben's story, *Breakaway Hearts*. If you did, please leave a review on the site where you purchased this book or on Goodreads.

I love to hear from readers. You can find me on Facebook and Twitter, or you can email me using the contact form on my website, www.CristaMcHugh.com.

If you would like to be the first to know about new releases or be entered into exclusive contests, please sign up for my newsletter using the contact form on my website.

Also, please like my Facebook page for more excerpts and teasers from upcoming books.

--Crista

Don't miss the next book in the Kelly Brothers series....

Breakaway Hearts

Hockey star Ben Kelly retreats to his mountain cabin in the ski town of Cascade, BC, to recuperate from a season-ending knee injury and contemplate his future in the NHL. He never expects to run into the one woman who got away. Nine years may have passed, but nothing has dulled the explosive chemistry between them. Now he wants more than just one night.

Hailey Eriksson had Olympic-sized dreams until an accidental pregnancy from a one-night stand halted her ambitions. Her life was shattered when her son died. Nothing will keep her from fulfilling her promise to him to make the Olympic team, especially not the charming Ben Kelly. Unfortunately, he's out to sweep her off her feet this time, and she finds him harder and harder to resist with each passionate kiss. But when he learns about the child he never knew, will their rekindled romance be on thin ice?

Coming February 3, 2014

Books by Crista McHugh

The Kelly Brothers
The Sweetest Seduction, Book 1
Breakaway Hearts, Book 2
Falling for the Wingman, Book 3 (Mar. 2014)
The Heart's Game, Book 4 (July 2014)

The Soulbearer Trilogy
A Soul For Trouble
A Soul For Chaos
A Soul For Vengeance

The Elgean Chronicles:
A Thread of Magic
The Tears of Elios

The Deizian Empire:
Tangled Web
Poisoned Web
Deception's Web

The Kavanaugh Foundation:
Heart of a Huntress, Book 1
Angelic Surrender, Book 2
"A High Stakes Game", Book 2.5 (a free read)
Kiss of Temptation, Book 3
Night of the Huntress (Print Anthology of Books 1 and 2)

Other titles by Crista McHugh
The Alchemy of Desire
"A Waltz at Midnight"
Cat's Eyes
"More Than a Fling"
"Provoking the Spirit"
Eight Tiny Flames (part of *A Very Scandalous Holiday* Anthology)

Author Bio:

Growing up in small town Alabama, Crista relied on story-telling as a natural way for her to pass the time and keep her two younger sisters entertained.

She currently lives in the Audi-filled suburbs of Seattle with her husband and two children, maintaining her alter ego of mild-mannered physician by day while she continues to pursue writing on nights and weekends.

Just for laughs, here are some of the jobs she's had in the past to pay the bills: barista, bartender, sommelier, stagehand, actress, morgue attendant, and autopsy assistant.

And she's also a recovering LARPer. (She blames it on her crazy college days)

For the latest updates, deleted scenes, and answers to any burning questions you have, please check out her webpage, www.CristaMcHugh.com.

Find Crista online at:
Twitter: twitter.com/crista_mchugh
Facebook: www.facebook.com/CristaMcHugh